I0594311

For all the authors writing the stories helping everyone
escape right now. You rock.

A FOUR ARTS NOVELLA

COURTING THE WITCH

M.J. SCOTT

Chapter One

Lieutenant Imogene Carvelle held on to the leather strap that was all that was keeping her from being bounced off the unyielding seat of the charguerre and wished devoutly to be anywhere else.

Three weeks of one uncomfortable, too hot or too cold, bone-shaking conveyance after another to return to Lumia from Reyshaka. She did not begrudge her emperor, His Imperial Majesty Aristides Delmar de Lucien, her services—in fact, she was most grateful for the opportunities and adventures it had afforded her thus far—but she remained baffled that his Imperial Army could not come up with some more comfortable modes of long-distance transportation. At least now that they were back in Illvya, the weather was far more pleasant than the icy conditions in the empire's far north.

The charguerre shuddered to a halt, and the door opened. "Last break before Lumia. Do what you will," one of the sergeants bellowed, and her squad companions began to climb out, muttering various degrees of complaint and relief. She was last to leave the charguerre and she headed straight for the queue that would be forming for tea and whatever the last of their food supplies was to fuel the remaining three hours to the city. Her other squad mates would be gossiping or finding a handy spot to relieve themselves or taking time to stretch their legs, but she wanted nothing more than tea and a few minutes in the relative quiet of the countryside before having to climb back into the noisy iron box that was the charguerre. She joined the end of the queue and, while she waited, sent her magic seeking down for a ley line. It took a minute or so to find the closest one. It was weak, but she pulled a little power, using the magic to chase away some of the fatigue making her bones ache.

"Are you looking forward to being home, Lieutenant?"

She blinked up at the speaker. Captain Honore Brodier was regular army, not part of the Imperial Mages as Imogene was, and one of the leaders of the company who had escorted the mages on their diplomatic mission. She was tall and blonde, showing her Elenian ancestral roots in the glacial blue of her eyes. Some of the squad called her, unoriginally, the Ice Queen, but she had always been kind to Imogene.

But the question, well-intentioned as Honore may be, was difficult to answer. "It will be nice to see my family," Imogene said as they stepped closer to the wooden trestle table that held hastily heated kettles of water.

"Keen to get back out, are you?" Honore said with a smile. She had a few years on Imogene's twenty-four, and the experience to go with them.

"Yes," Imogene said. There was no point denying it. She'd spent her first year in the Imperial mages doing mainly desk work and standard magic at one of the army's administrative centers just outside Lumia. She'd put her head down, worked hard, and won the respect of her captain, who'd recommended her for the Diplomatic Corps she'd been so eager to join. Her first mission had been a diplomatic assignment like this one—to Andalyssia, a part of the empire no more warm, though supposedly less wild than Reyshaka.

She wasn't sure she agreed with that assessment. The Andalyssians had been aloof, the magic they practiced bound up in a worship of nature that was somehow ponderous and secretive. Even thinking of it now, she could smell the moss and peat and salted ash that perfumed the court, an aroma from the ritual fires they burned continuously that seemed to permeate the entire frigid country. The magic she'd caught glimpses of seemed smoke-wreathed and heavy. The Andalyssians recognized earth and water and air and blood in their magic, as Illvya did, but they did not use them in the same way. Their ley lines were deep and old and resistant to Imogene's attempts to tap that power in a way that had made her glad there were soldiers as well as diplomats on that mission. A mission plagued by disasters and headed by a fool who no longer served His Imperial Majesty. Not that any of it had been Imogene's fault, but the army had shunted her into six months of boring, short-term courier assignments before deciding she'd done her time and could try again. It had seemed an eternity while she waited for the stink of disaster—which might always be linked to those Andalyssian memories—to clear from her.

Reyshaka had been a second chance. One she'd seized. She liked to think she'd succeeded in her duties. And, despite the discomforts of the climate, she'd found it fascinating.

She was very much hoping not to get stuck in Lumia again for more than a few weeks, if only because being stationed so close to home would give her mother more opportunities to tout the wonders of marriage and plot Imogene's betrothal. Imogene's two older sisters were both married, as was her brother, and her youngest sister had just become engaged. Which left Imogene as the sole target of her mother's match-making tendencies.

As much as she missed her family and her friends—her best friend, Chloe Matin, in particular —she was not yet keen to settle down. Not when she'd just begun seeing some of the corners of the empire she'd grown up reading about.

She accepted tea as Honore said, "I'll be glad of a rest. This is my ninth extended mission in a row. Sometimes I think my backside will never regain feeling."

They both turned and looked at the line of solid square charguerres and the chunky fer-taureaus that pulled them, grimacing in unison. The fer-taureaus were modeled after iron bulls, but they looked about as much like actual bulls as the charguerre did like carriages. And their gait was less graceful than any real animal.

"Your father is an ingenier, is he not?" Honore asked. "Maybe when you get home, you should ask him how to make those damned things more comfortable."

"An ingenier, but not a mage ingenier. I asked him once. He said he would have to inspect one to know what might be possible. But he thought it would be difficult to improve the ride much without altering the structure in ways that might weaken them."

"We're doomed, then," Honore said, pushing her free hand into the small of her back. "Maybe I should try for a sea voyage next. Ships don't bounce."

Imogene shrugged, smiling. "They roll, though. And sink. And there's always more travel when you disembark." And ships were still slow. Even the fastest courier craft were at the mercy of the ocean and the winds.

The part of her that was her father's daughter stowed the problem away to chew on at another time. She was a diplomat, not a mage ingenier, and in another three hours, she would be home in Lumia. Where she would be putting in the work to make sure she stayed a diplomat.

She stared back at the charguerres. Cesarus, the familiaris sanctii bonded to Major Fontaine, the senior mage for this mission, was standing near the last one in the line. He was very still, as was his nature, but Imogene thought she'd caught his eye and waved as she would to any other member of the squad.

The sanctii nodded back.

"You do well with them," Honore observed. "Have you thought of bonding one yourself?"

Imogene blinked, startled. Sanctii fascinated her as much as diplomacy. They always had, since she'd first lived with them at the Academe di Sages. But while she was a water mage, and technically any water mage was free to bond a sanctii, it was an unwritten rule that an Imperial mage would not do so without permission. Such permission usually only came with seniority. "I'm a little young, I think."

Honore shrugged, sipped her tea. "Old enough, perhaps. You have a talent for this work. You did well in Reyshaka."

And sanctii were useful to diplomats. They could be used to spy, to intimidate, or to fascinate. Or to protect.

"It's something I had considered might be possible in the future," Imogene said carefully, hiding her pleasure at the praise and her excitement at even a hint that she might be able to bond a sanctii.

Cool blue eyes studied her. "The major and I would be happy to make a recommendation. Should you want to move that future somewhat nearer." Honore swigged the last of her tea. "But you don't need to decide now. No doubt you are tired and longing for a bath, as I am. Come see me in a day or so and let me know." She handed the mug back to the waiting orderly and tugged her uniform jacket straighter, clearly preparing to move on to whatever was next on her mental list of tasks to complete in this break.

"I will. Thank you, Captain." She hoped the excitement and apprehension suddenly fizzing through her veins wasn't too apparent. "I appreciate your confidence in me."

Honore smiled, but then her expression turned serious. "Just keep your nose clean. I know that mess with Alexei had nothing to do with you, and you've proven yourself here, but the army has a long memory."

Chapter Two

✣

"So was it wonderful?"

Imogene looked over at Chloe Matin, who was currently bouncing on Imogene's bed in a manner which would make Imogene's mama, should she walk into the room right now, tell them both they were acting like children. It was always strange to return to her parents' home after the freedom of a mission. Being back under their roof, in the same bed she'd slept in since childhood, gave her an odd sense of being caught between her past and her future. Though Chloe, her best friend for many years, was always welcome wherever Imogene was.

"Stop bouncing and I might tell you. Better still, start passing me things out of that trunk." She waved her hand at the battered wood and iron trunk near the bed.

On Chloe's arrival, Imogen had shooed Dina, the Carvelles' maid, away, preferring to talk in private. Dina had obeyed after removing all the clothes that required washing—which, after the long journey home, was most of the contents of the trunk. But some had survived Dina's inspection and deemed clean. Which left Imogene with the task of rehanging them and unpacking the other bits and pieces she had taken with her.

Chloe slithered off the bed, kneeling beside the trunk and peering into it to see what remained. "Well?"

Imogene shoved aside two silk ball gowns that were distinctly not the type of clothes she preferred—and she was dreading her mother's explanation as to why they had appeared in her wardrobe—and tucked her sole clean uniform jacket into place before turning back to Chloe, who promptly handed her a pair of boots.

"It was...intriguing. And exhausting. Fascinating. And nerve-racking." She grinned at Chloe. "I can't wait to do it all over again." She bent to put the boots away. When she straightened, Chloe's expression had turned gloomy.

"So you're definitely going to ask for another assignment, then?" Chloe asked.

Imogene hesitated. Chloe, a year younger than Imogene, wanted to join the Imperial Corps, too. But her mother had fallen ill not long after Chloe turned twenty-one and manifested her magic, and Chloe had temporarily given up her plans to help her family out. "Temporarily" had stretched to several years already. Chloe had completed her studies—her father was the Maistre of the Academe di Sages, after all—but spent all the time she could running the Matin household and looking after her younger brother and sister.

"How is your mama?" Imogene asked gently. They'd written to each other while she had been away, but Chloe had kept her letters relentlessly positive and gossipy, so Imogene didn't know what the actual situation might be.

Chloe's smile was a little too cheerful. "She continues to improve. We are hopeful she will be fully well again within the year."

In other words, Chloe would not be joining up this year either. And might not like Imogene's response. But Imogene wasn't about to start lying to her best friend.

"I am planning to ask for another assignment. I don't think I'll be in town very long." Too long and her mother would start getting ideas. The Carvelles weren't part of the level of society that partook in the palace's season of balls and entertainments that were prime matchmaking territory for the Illvyan nobility, but there were similar events amongst the families of the well-off merchants and such. Her mother had, no doubt, already made a list in triplicate of potential suitors, as she had every year since Imogene turned twenty-one. There was no other explanation for the new ball gowns.

"So we must spend time together while we can," she continued, reaching for Chloe's hand, squeezing it.

Chloe looked away. Then she lifted her chin, another of those too-bright smiles stretched across her face. "Speaking of which, Father has an invitation to the imperial ball this week. Mother cannot attend, so he asked permission to bring me. And a friend. Will you come?"

To a palace ball? Her mother would go into a frenzy. "It's not really—"

"Oh don't be boring. It will be fun," Chloe said. "In fact, it's the perfect way to outwit your mother. None of the aristocratic bachelors will be looking for anything serious with the likes of us, so you can flirt and dance in perfect safety." She grinned then, dark brows lifted in challenge.

There was an argument Imogene hadn't considered. Chloe, as Henri's daughter and a strong witch, was perfectly eligible, as she herself was. But there were also plenty of women with power among the noble families. Most of the bachelors at an imperial ball would be on the hunt for someone with a title, or a dowry far more impressive than either she or Chloe could bring to the table, or trying to avoid matrimony altogether.

Chloe was right. Those men were safe. Those men might even offer the opportunity for the kind of entertainment she hadn't indulged in at all during her mission. Smart girls didn't have liaisons with members of their own squads. Or companies. She missed sex. In some parts of the empire—and in mysterious Anglion across the ocean—they had odd rules about such things, particularly for young witches or potential witches. Or so she had heard. Here in Illvya, other than perhaps in the highest families, the unwritten rules were "don't get pregnant and don't cause a scandal." Easy enough for a witch with the brains to choose a sensible, discreet partner, and to wield a basic knowledge of herbs and the ways of female and male bodies. So why not enjoy herself?

Captain Brodier had told her to keep her nose clean. That meant stay out of the spotlight, not avoid fun altogether.

Furthermore, if she was at a palace ball, she couldn't be at one of the balls she suspected her mother would be forcing her to attend where the men were far more likely to be looking for a wife like her and therefore apt to become troublesome.

She threw an arm around Chloe and kissed her cheek. "Darling one, I believe you're a genius. A ball sounds wonderful."

Chapter Three

The palace was lit up like a chandelier. Light streamed from every window, casting a shimmering golden hue over the white marble facade, making it look like something summoned from a dream. A floating, gleaming confection of magnificence defying the night.

Imogen knew the size and scope of the palace, the arc of its marble and gilt and glass designed to shout power and might to the world. She knew the less grand administrative buildings in the complex of barracks, office, workshops, and stables that nestled behind the palace best but had some familiarity with the public parts of the palace itself. But its beauty tonight left her almost giddy as the Matins' carriage drew closer to the head of the queue of carriages waiting to deliver their occupants to the ball.

She flexed her hands in their white satin gloves and tried to draw a deep breath. The corset she wore under her sapphire blue gown made that difficult. She'd made Dina lace it as loosely as possible, but the truth of the matter was that the dresses her mother had ordered were cut tight, and "loosely" was a relative term. The corsets she wore with her uniforms were sensible, front lacing so she could get herself in and out of her clothes, and comfort-able as old shoes. She'd forgotten the restrictions of formal gowns.

What would Honore think if she saw Imogene now?

Imogene had told the captain the previous day that yes, she would like to be recommended to bond a sanctii. Honore had seemed pleased, though she repeated her warnings about behaving.

Perhaps that was part of the reason she was so excited now. She hadn't told anyone—not even Chloe—she had a chance at a sanctii, and she had no intention of doing so until she'd been formally granted permission. And really, an invitation to a ball at the palace was respectable in all senses of the word. Her dress was tight, but it was not in any way scandalous. Her mother, annoying as she could be, had undeniable style—even if her choices might not always be Imogene's—and would never send her daughter out in a dress of questionable taste.

She made herself take a breath, then settle back against the seat and try to relax. Enjoy the mo-ment. Choose a night of froth and bubble to let herself shine after months of being the sober, somber lieutenant. Indulge in being female and enjoy the ritual of Dina doing her hair and pulling out her makeup and choosing jewelry to sparkle and gleam at ear and wrist and throat. But there was a limit to how far one could relax in a corset laced for a ball gown. Froth and bubble were all very well, but why couldn't they be a little more comfortable?

"Ready, girls?" Henri Matin asked as the car-riage inched forward. Imogene was used to seeing Chloe's father in his Academe robes. In his evening clothes—more formal even than what he wore to the occasional party in their circles—he looked debonair but still mysterious. His sanctii, Martius, was nowhere to be seen. Which didn't mean he wasn't nearby. Sanctii could be invisible and incorporeal when they chose.

Perhaps it was just as well he wasn't riding in the carriage. She might do something foolish and give her excitement away if she was too close to a sanctii just now. She knew Martius as well as a mage could know any sanctii not their own, and he sometimes chose to speak to her. It would be tempting to ask him more about his kind. But even if Henri had not been present, there was the risk that Martius would report any conversation he had back to Henri. For now, Imogene needed to stay silent and rely on the knowledge from her studies. She'd managed to find several of her old textbooks buried in a storage box under her bed and refreshed herself on the lore of sanctii. But none of them contained the actual details of a bonding. Such things were deemed too risky for students. There were books that did contain the information, of course, but she'd had no chance to find a bookstore that might sell them and no excuse to return to the Academe and dig through its library. Besides, she suspected the army would have its own preferences for how the rituals should be performed.

"Of course we're ready," Chloe said, dragging Imogene's attention back to the here and now.

Henri grinned fondly at her. "The more pertinent question may be whether the palace is ready for the two of you, I suspect. Promise me you will behave. Mostly."

Chloe glanced at her father and raised her eyebrows. "Of course, Papa. When have you known us to get into trouble?"

"Only most days of your lives," Henri said. "But this is the palace. There are rules here. You can have fun, dance, flirt with the men who want to flirt with you, but don't forget who you're dealing with. The emperor keeps a tight rein on his court, but most people inside these walls are playing games of power. Don't become pawns."

"No one will be very interested in us," Imogene said. At least, not for the kinds of games Henri was thinking of. She had a different kind in mind.

"Two young, beautiful, strong witches? There may be more interest than you think. Perhaps not from the aristos, but there will be parliamentarians and courtiers and all sorts of men looking to rise high. Don't underestimate them or what they might do." His brows, starting to show threads of gray amongst the black, drew together. "You are here with me, and that will offer a degree of protection, but keep your wits about you."

He was, Imogene thought, being dramatic. Her time with the mages had left her well-trained in how to deal with unwanted advances, and she intended to be less than interesting to any men who showed even the slightest tendency toward matrimony.

"We'll stick together," Imogene said, exchanging a look with Chloe. She hadn't asked Chloe if there was anyone in particular she was hoping to meet at the ball. Hopefully she wasn't about to ruin any...fun Chloe had arranged for herself.

Her friend had maintained her determinedly cheerful face every time they'd seen each other in the three days since Chloe had issued her invitation, but Imogene saw the tension beneath it all. Though so far, Chloe had resisted Imogene's attempts to give her an opening to talk about how she felt. Imogene had to respect that choice.

And she would do so. Along with doing her best to aid Chloe in anything she might choose to do to indulge herself for a night. If anyone deserved fun, it was Chloe. So if that meant distracting Henri from his daughter's choices, or putting her own plans on hold, she would.

Chloe's dress was the shade of ripe seila berries. The deep red set off her pale skin and dark eyes beautifully. She was taller than Imogene, and her figure ran more to curves. She'd be beating off the young aristos with a stick if she chose.

Imogene's own dress was her favorite shade of sapphire blue. Her mother had gotten that much right. And Imogene was hoping it might, when the carriage finally reached the front entrance to the palace, help her do some aristo fishing of her own.

Chapter Four

Jean-Paul du Laq watched the whirling throng of dancers decorating the emperor's ballroom and wished there was something stronger than campenois on offer to drink. An imperial ball was never his first choice of entertainment—too many damned people and too much politicking for it to be actual fun—but as the heir of a duq, sometimes duty took precedence over his own wishes. His father was not yet old and, goddess willing, there would be years before Jean-Paul had to assume the title, but lately, duty was encroaching more and more often.

From his father came more demands to show his face at the palace and take his place in the court, when in reality, Jean-Paul was far happier serving in the army or spending his spare time at the family's estate, Sanct de Sangre. That side of being a duq—the running of the estate, seeing the land and the people flourish under his family's care —he would enjoy when it became his turn. This part—the social whirl and posturing and scrambling for power—he was yet to develop much of a liking for.

He appreciated the view, to a degree. Watching beautiful women in beautiful gowns was never a hardship. He would have enjoyed it more if his father's speeches about carrying on the family line weren't growing more frequent. He was only twenty-eight. Plenty of time before marriage grew pressing. But he knew that some of the women here tonight—and their parents—would be watching him. Trying to determine how to win his favor. The son of a duq, heir to one of the oldest titles in Illvya, was a prize.

But he was in no mood to be hunted. So lurking on the outskirts of the room where Aristides's servants had placed thick rows of anden trees in golden and silver inlaid pots was the wiser course of action. The trees helped him blend in. He was taller than most of the men here, and the black and silver of his evening jacket only made his height more apparent. But sons of duqs weren't allowed to slouch or dress to blend in, so he had no choice but to stand out in most crowds.

"Hiding in the bushes again, du Laq?" Theodor du Plesias asked, gliding up from behind him.

"Not well enough if you found me," Jean-Paul retorted.

Teddy grinned and held up a slender glass bottle filled with pale green liquid. "Thought you might need a drop of something stronger than campenois."

"I knew there was a reason I tolerated you," Jean-Paul said. He held out his empty glass. Teddy poured in a careful measure. Absintia was potent. It could cause actual harm if brewed incorrectly, or if you drank it like wine. But he trusted Teddy to have the good stuff. And Jean-Paul would avoid a second glass. He couldn't afford for his wits to be addled. Not when the room was full of husband-hunters and their mamas.

The absintia was herbal fire as it coated his throat and stomach but soon resolved into a pleasant warmth that melted away some of his boredom.

"So, can I coax you out of the bushes?" Teddy asked. "It's a dull way to spend an evening in a room full of pretty girls."

"Easy for you to say. No one is forcing you to marry and carry on the dynasty." Teddy was a third son. His father, the Marq of Elimen, already had five grandchildren and counting from Teddy's elder brothers. Which left Teddy largely free of the kinds of parental pressures Jean-Paul was becoming uncomfortably familiar with.

"Marriage is not on my mind," Teddy agreed amiably. "But that doesn't mean female company isn't. There are some interesting girls here tonight. Aristides invited some of the senior mages and their families, and some of the parliamentarians, too." He waved his glass of absintia out toward the dancers. "Some of them must be looking for some fun."

He had a point. Jean-Paul had no intention of going after a politician's daughter. Too close to a courtier. But the mages were safer. And young witches from outside the nobility were raised with rather a more liberal mindset in relation to male companionship than the girls he'd known since infancy. But, with the absintia lifting his mood, dancing sounded more pleasant. And if dancing led to more, should the lady be willing, even better.

"Do you know where these paragons of, er, congeniality might be found?" he inquired, placing his glass in the pot of the nearest tree.

Teddy laughed and beckoned him forward, closer to the dancers. Jean-Paul had chosen the rear of the ballroom, far away from the area kept cordoned off for the imperial family and their chosen guests. The perfect vantage point from which to survey the entire ballroom. Helped by the fact that his height allowed him to see over the crowd with ease.

Teddy, only an inch or two shorter than Jean-Paul, gestured across the room. "There, the girl in the deep red dress. That's Chloe Matin, Henri's daughter."

Jean-Paul found the girl—young woman—Teddy meant. Her gown, the pinkish-red of good wine, wrapped around a very nice set of curves, highlighting creamy skin and blending with the touches of red and black in her hair. But then she stepped to one side, and he saw the woman standing next to her. She wore blue that gleamed like the finest sapphire and, as she turned to laugh up at something Chloe had said, the angles of her face caught his eye and held it. Her hair was darker than Chloe's, the original deep brown of it still twined with the red and black streaks that proclaimed her to be an earth witch and a water mage, like her friend. Her skin was paler than Chloe's, too, cool pearl against the blue. And her eyes, well, those were as bright as her gown. She looked across the room toward him, but her gaze flicked past him with no sign of recognition. But the brief touch of that look sizzled through him like lightning.

"Who," he breathed, "is the one in blue?"

Teddy's brows drew down as he contemplated the question. "Imogene...something. She's in the mages, apparently. Friend of the Matin lass."

"Which part of the mages?" Jean-Paul asked. He wasn't sure what he'd thought someone so...vivid might do for a living, but the army wouldn't have been his first choice.

Teddy shrugged. "I don't know." He nudged Jean-Paul's ribs with his elbow. "Perhaps that's a question for the lady herself. If she's caught your eye."

Jean-Paul was still watching Imogene, too riveted by her still to react to Teddy's jab—either the physical or verbal one.

"She has, hasn't she?" Teddy said with another nudge. "Good choice. A career girl, if she's in the mages. She won't give you any grief."

Jean-Paul didn't really register the words, but he knew what Teddy meant. A mage—a career soldier —would know how things worked. She wouldn't be after marriage. Might be amenable to a dalliance to burn out this fire leaping in his gut and speeding his heart.

He ignored the part of him that had a vague notion that a heat like this might not be so easy to douse and stepped out onto the dance floor.

Chapter Five

Imogene accepted a glass of campenois from a circulating servant, waving her fan idly in her other hand. The ballroom was becoming, as ballrooms always did, overly warm now that the dancing was underway. She was glad to sit out the current round of dances. The emperor's ballroom was large, but so was the number of people filling it. She'd wanted another drink more than she wanted to dance her way through the crush with the last nervous young aristo who'd approached her, so she'd declined him with a smile designed to be both firm and politely demure, pleading a need to retire temporarily. He'd shrugged and moved on to another group of young ladies, not seeming fazed by the refusal.

The pale blonde in bright yellow he'd asked next had accepted, and Imogene had watched them join the dancers before she'd made her way back toward Chloe. She had no idea how many people were in attendance, but it would be easy enough to lose someone in the crush. She and Chloe had agreed to stay close while they got the lay of the land, so to speak. Imogene had spotted a few faces she recognized from the Imperial mages and the Academe, as well as the odd aristocrat or politician, but those had been few and far between so far. She needed to take some time, gather some information, before she made any choices that might lead to something more than being steered around the dance floor.

She'd so far danced with four of the men who'd asked. Two had been pleasant, but nothing more than that, and the third dull. The fourth had earned himself a well-stomped set of toes when he'd attempted to let his hand drift farther down her back than was acceptable, given she'd offered no encouragement for him to take liberties and that they were in a very public place. That would be another benefit if she bonded with a sanctii—handy for dealing with wayward suitors.

Illvyans, on the whole, didn't have the ill-informed superstitions and fear of sanctii that some of the other countries in the empire—and beyond—did, but they still viewed them with a healthy degree of respect. Or the ones who had any brains did. Of course, she couldn't say for sure that the young man in question met that criterion.

That was the problem with balls. There was no time to converse with a man before having to accept or decline an invitation to dance. No time to judge his intelligence or personality before being stuck with him for the duration of a set.

She needed a different strategy. Retreat from the dancing and try to find men who were keeping farther afield of the festivities to talk to. Of course, that would mean abandoning Chloe, who loved to dance.

She glanced over at her friend, who was happily talking with several other men and women their age and didn't look as though she needed any assistance.

Good. With Chloe occupied, Imogene was free to explore for a while and see what she might find in the quieter parts of this ball. If such places existed.

But before she could decide which direction she might try first, there was a minor commotion to her right, and she looked up to see a man—or perhaps a small mountain—striding through one of the sets of dancers, moving in her direction.

A sensible person would have backed away. He really was unreasonably tall and wide and looked capable of flattening anyone in his path. The dancers dispersing to either side of him seemed to have formed the same conclusion. But Imogene, instead of being sensible, found herself unable to look away. He wasn't just tall. There was strength to go with the height—not even the excellent work of his tailor could hide the powerful lines of his body completely and make him look like a tame courtier. But he was more than any other well-built man. No, he was more...arresting than that.

His face was carved from planes and angles that shouldn't have added up to pleasing but somehow did. His hair was black—curly, possibly, if it hadn't been tied back. His eyes, well, she couldn't tell yet if they were blue or gray or something in between from where she stood. And the only thing about his eyes—whatever color they were—that seemed important was how firmly they were fixed on hers with the kind of intent determination that, again, would have made a sensible person retreat.

She couldn't look away. And had to fight a startling desire to walk to meet him.

It would have been easy to do. A path was rapidly clearing in front of him, as though a blood mage had cast a spear of power straight across the room to push people out of his way. But she saw no sign of magic. It was just self-preservation on the part of those moving. And, she realized, as heads began to turn in her direction to see where this mountain of a man was headed, self-preservation was fast being replaced by curiosity for those who had made it safely out of his way.

She lifted her chin. Most of the people at the ball had no idea who she was. Which was fine by her. The life of a courtier had never been her goal.

The mystery man was getting closer. And his gaze didn't break from hers. Her dress felt too tight, as though Dina had just freshly tugged on her corset strings. Her breath didn't want to come easily, and she was suddenly far too aware of how overheated the room was.

Ten feet away. Five. A step more. He stopped there. She just had time to register that his eyes were indeed a thunderous shade of gray before he swept into a flawless bow.

So flawless he had to be nobility. Only one raised to court from birth would have that degree of effortless perfection in his gestures.

As he straightened, she dipped into her best curtsy. It might not have been as perfect as his, but she fancied she managed it gracefully enough. Diplomats were also schooled in manners, after all. Reyshaka utilized a complicated system of bows with matching hand positions depending on gender, rank, and age for both sexes, so it was something of a relief to return to the simplicity of a curtsy, even though executing it did nothing to ease her breathlessness.

When she rose, he was smiling at her as though she were his favorite dessert. Behind him, interested faces were peering in their direction.

"My lady, may I be so bold as to introduce myself?"

She snapped her fan open, pretending to consider. She wanted to know his name. From the interest of the courtiers, he was clearly someone important. "I suppose I might as well make the inconvenience of all those dancers you displaced serve some purpose and say yes."

His smile widened. "Excellent. I am Jean-Paul du Laq."

He didn't add any titles. He didn't need to. She didn't know the name of every minor nobleman who decorated the court—it wasn't required for her current rank in the mages—but she was well versed in the names of the highest families. After all, some of them passed through the Academe di Sages where she had done her schooling—schooling which included many hours of the history of the empire and those who'd done the conquering—and a number of them graced the ranks of the Imperial mages. And even without that, anyone who read the news sheet stories about court life could hardly fail to know who was who in the upper ranks of nobility.

Du Laq was the family name of the Duq of San Pierre. The only way to hold a higher rank would be to be a member of the royal family itself. They were a family as old as the bones of the empire and had served generations of emperors.

And the name of the oldest son of the Duq of San Pierre was Jean-Paul.

Chapter Six

✦

Well. That was convenient. The son of a duq —what's more, the heir himself—might very well serve her purpose of finding a man to share her bed for a night with no risk of entanglement, even though she may not have thought of setting her sights so high.

That he was the very handsome son of a duq was even better. A man of his rank wouldn't be looking for anything more than a dalliance with someone like her.

The likes of him didn't marry women who came from very middling families like hers. Not if they had no dazzling dowry to make up for the lack of rank. Though the du Laq family didn't need money. Unlike some noble families, they held firmly to their power and grew their fortunes with the same level of determination.

But even so, families like his married their own kind.

Which she was not. Though with his gaze still heating her skin, she thought they had, perhaps, at least some level of... connection. Even if it was the most basic kind.

"I see I have stunned you to silence," he said

dryly, breaking the silence her whirring thoughts had stretched too long.

"My pardon, my lord. I was trying to recollect your title but cannot bring it to mind." Most courtiers would rather die than admit such a thing. But she wanted him to be clear about who she was. And that his title was of no use to her other than to render her safe from a man seeking something serious.

Anything that might come after would be entered into with no misunderstandings. She smiled at him to emphasize the fact that she had no shame about her lack of recollection. "But I am pleased to meet you, regardless."

"And I am very glad to hear that." His eyes, now that they were so close, proved to be not only gray but full of mischief. "And may I have the pleasure of knowing your name, Mamsille?"

She folded her fan again. He was, when you got right down to it, breaking protocol to speak to her without an introduction. As long as they continued to entertain each other in this conversation, she didn't think it would take any particular convoluted method of flirtation to get to the point. "Lieutenant Imogene Carvelle," she said. One of his brows lifted, and his gaze drifted down. Looking for a ring on her hand, perhaps? Wise. By telling him her title instead of repeating his "Mamsille" or correcting him to "Madame," she'd avoided confirming his assumption that she was unmarried.

Her hands were bare except for the black pearl ring she wore on the index finger of her right hand —a gift from her parents when she'd manifested her magic.

Indeed, that seemed to please him. His smile widened as his gaze lifted. "Ah, a soldier. Which regiment?" His tone was distinctly approving.

"I'm in the mages," she said, not wanting to

provide him with too much information immediately.

Another lift of that very dark brow. "I haven't
seen you before."

"You're in the mages?" She couldn't remember
meeting him. And he would have been difficult to
forget. Belatedly she thought to look for his magic,
but if he had any, he wasn't using it. She saw no
connection to the ley line that ran beneath the
palace and none of the glittering colors dancing
over his skin, which was how she usually saw magic.

"No, just the regulars." He shrugged. "I have a
little magic but not enough to be of interest to the
mages. Fortunately, I have other talents."

Plus no lack of confidence, it seemed. That
went with being the son of a duq, she supposed.
And, truthfully, it wasn't unattractive. His tone
wasn't smug, just matter-of-fact and, unless she was
mistaken, somewhat flirtatious. She smiled back at
him. "I'm sure you do, my lord."

His nose wrinkled. "Jean-Paul, please."

"That is hardly proper on such a formal
occasion."

"It's a ball. The purpose of a ball is to let people
socialize and get to know one another, surely?"

"I always thought a large part of the purpose of
imperial balls was to get nobles such as yourself
safely married off." She looked pointedly down at
his hand so he'd understand she'd noticed his inspection earlier. The long, tanned fingers were
bare. "Is that why you're here, my lord?"

"I'm sure it's why my parents wish I was here,"
he said. "But no, Lieutenant, I have no particular
desire to rush headlong into marriage. My father is
young and healthy, and I have siblings should something unfortunate happen to me. I'm here to enjoy
myself. Drink some campenois, dance with some

pretty women. Would you grant me a dance, Lieutenant?" He proffered a hand.

She stifled the immediate instinct to reach out and take it. "Is one of your talents dancing, my lord?"

"I get no complaints," he said. "And a new set is forming." He crooked his fingers. "You wouldn't want us to be late."

"I haven't said yes yet," she pointed out.

"You haven't said no either. I'll take that as a promising sign."

"You, my lord, may be overly sure of yourself."

"Perhaps. But that doesn't mean you don't want to dance with me."

He had her there. Because she did want to dance with him. Wanted to feel his hand on hers and see if moving with him to the music was as fun as this initial conversation had been. After months of familiar squad members and politics in the Reyshakan court, which had involved just about the opposite of flirtation, his attention was somewhat dizzying.

So, in the mood to be a little giddy, she reached out and took his hand.

Chapter Seven

Jean-Paul du Laq may have crossed the ballroom like a mountain on a mission, but he definitely didn't dance like one.

No, being on the dance floor with him, strong, warm fingers wrapped around her hand and touching her waist, was perhaps more like being swept around the room in the eye of a storm. She had the oddest sensation of something swirling around her, huge and important and wild, but also of perfect stillness as she stared up into smiling gray eyes and let him lead. Just her luck that the orchestra had decided this was to be a set of waltzes rather than some of the statelier Illvyan dances, where she would have had time to step away from him now and then to catch her breath and to let her brain regain control.

Instead, she whirled around with him, barely aware of the music, somewhat breathless from more than the fit of her dress and completely unable to stop herself from smiling with delight.

Perhaps he was an illusioner, this son of a duq? He'd claimed to have little magic, but that could be a lie. A way to disarm an unsuspecting female so he could work some sort of dazzlement. But she saw no spark of magic around him, none of the glimmering haze of power that marked a mage at work to her eyes. So there was nothing to blame for this giddiness but the man himself.

The music started to slow as the musicians began the transition to the next dance, and Jean-Paul eased their pace. Unfortunately, he also pulled her closer. Not more than was acceptable in public, but close enough that she could feel him radiating heat and smell warm linen and warm man.

A scent she wanted more of. But no. She bit down on her instinct to close the gap between them farther still and forced herself to speak. "So, my lord, you said you were in the regulars? What exactly do you do?"

"I'm in the centiene."

Hardly the regulars. The centiene were the emperor's elite cavalry. Which made sense for a man of his rank. She tried to picture a warhorse large enough to carry him comfortably and felt her mouth quirk again. Not a beast she would like to tangle with.

"Captain?" she ventured. Her brain was failing to provide his age or his exact title. Older than her, she thought, but less than thirty. There were no gray threads in his hair, and while the lines by his eyes crinkled attractively when he smiled, she judged them to be from time outdoors, not age.

"Major," he corrected.

"Impressive," she said. Either he was very, very good at command or he was older than she would have guessed.

"Did you think I was a dilettante who had purchased a commission on the merits of my family's name rather than earning my command?"

"My lord, I have not known you long enough to judge, but no, you do not strike me as anything but competent." He was hardly the languid, foppish sort of aristo who largely seemed to spend money rather than do anything to earn it that she had sometimes encountered. He was the scion of an ancient family. Destined to lead and protect. She doubted he had been raised to be anything but determined and accomplished.

"Are you judging that by my dancing?" His hand tightened, and he twirled them faster, completing two full rotations where the dance only called for one.

"That, my lord, sounds like you are fishing for compliments. Does your ego require reinforcing?"

The laugh that was his answer boomed across the ballroom.

Impressively, roaring with laughter didn't make the man skip a beat of the dance.

"Not usually, Lieutenant, but perhaps after a few hours in your company, I may need time to recover from being so neatly skewered." He grinned at her.

She doubted much could skewer this man. "A few hours, my lord? I don't think the set will last so long."

"There will be another set after this one. If you are inclined only to dancing."

Definitely not skewered. No dint to his confidence for him to be hinting at perhaps the chance for more. Some women would have thought him presumptuous. Or outright overstepping the bounds of good manners. Whereas she was just...well, judging by the heartbeat ringing in her ears at the thought of his hands touching other parts of her body, inclined to something more than dancing. But that didn't mean she would give in so easily.

"And if I were inclined only to dancing, my lord, would you still want to spend a few hours in my company?"

His expression turned thoughtful for a moment, and she wondered if he was going to say no. But then his hand tightened on her waist, just a fraction. Enough to draw her an inch closer, as though he rejected the notion of letting her go. "As it turns out, Lieutenant," he said, his eyes intent on hers, "I think I would."

She lost her breath. And perhaps her mind. The room continued to spin around them as they danced on, and she kept her eyes locked to Jean-Paul's. He seemed like the one true thing in the world. A sensation both reassuring and alarmingly seductive. A sensation she didn't want to come to an end. Not just yet. She needed to stay here where she could just dance and not think too hard. Not until she was sure she was ready to let him lead her on to the next step of this dance of theirs. She wanted what came after. Her body told her that. She ached to move closer to him. To touch more. To taste.

But a corner of her mind was also whispering that perhaps this was more than she'd gone looking for.

She didn't want to let that thought in. So instead she gazed into gray eyes that caught her like a storm and just danced.

And when they stood breathing hard after the set concluded, she decided that she would indeed chance the storm to see what happened. But, as Jean-Paul escorted her off the dance floor, there was a gold-and-silver-liveried servant waiting for him.

"Major," the man said. "I was sent to find you."

Imogene's heart dropped. Jean-Paul's hand, where it rested on hers tucked through his arm, flexed.

"My father?" Jean-Paul asked, sounding impatient.

"No, your emperor," the servant said.

Jean-Paul blew out a frustrated breath. She had some sympathy for that emotion. But he couldn't ignore the emperor's request.

She slid her arm free and stepped away. "You must go, my lord. Thank you for the dance."

He bowed fast and then straightened. "Don't go anywhere until I return, Lieutenant," he said fiercely, then caught her hand to his lips to kiss the back of her glove.

Chapter Eight

Jean-Paul followed the servant through the palace halls, recognizing the route toward one of Aristides's favorite audience chambers. That was a reassuring sign. If something had gone seriously wrong, he would have been ordered to the barracks to join the rest of his squad as soon as they'd left the ballroom. Mostly, though, he was aware that every step he took was in the wrong direction. He wanted to be back with Imogene, not doing whatever the hell this was. His body was rumbling with frustrated...well, he didn't want to think too closely on the sensation. Lust, yes. The woman was beautiful. But there was more than lust at play here. A thought perhaps, more disconcerting than why he was being dragged from the ballroom and her company.

But when the servant ushered him into the chamber with a discreet "The Marq of Lasienne" and he saw who stood talking with the emperor, his frustration at leaving Imogene and concern about what had happened to cause Aristides to drag him out of the ball was swamped by a pulse of deep irritation.

He bowed to Aristides with a quick "Your Imperial Majesty," then turned to greet the other man.

"Father. Fancy meeting you here." He tried to keep the impatience out of his voice and hoped to the goddess that this wasn't to be another of his father's "It's time to start paying more attention to your duties" talks, backed up with the weight of Aristides's presence.

"Jean-Paul." His father nodded a greeting. Dressed in a jacket embroidered with cresting waves in the du Laq blues, Andre du Laq glittered only slightly less than the emperor, whose jacket was a symphony of gold and silver. Knowing how much Aristides sometimes disliked the displays he was obliged to make, Jean-Paul could only imagine it had been chosen by the empress. "I hope you are enjoying the evening."

Well, he had been until now. But that wasn't a tactful response. Particularly when he didn't yet know what Aristides wanted.

He focused back on the emperor. Aristides was some eight years older than Jean-Paul, but they were friends of a kind. As much as you could be friends with an emperor. "You asked to see me, Your Imperial Majesty?"

"Yes," Aristides said. "I have a new assignment for you."

Jean-Paul's neck prickled. He wasn't sure he would like the next words out of Aristides's mouth. "I am, of course, happy to serve." Though somewhat confused. The emperor's Imperial Guard was run through the mage corps, not the regulars. Jean-Paul's military duties were assigned via his commanding officer, not Aristides.

"We have received word that the ambassadorial delegation from Andalyssia will reach the city tomorrow. I'd like you to oversee their security detail."

Security? Not usually the realm of the cavalry.

"Isn't that something the Guard should do?" he asked.

Aristides shrugged. "Things are still delicate with Andalyssia. We thought it best to make them feel as though we are paying them due deference. And so—" He pointed at Jean-Paul. "—they get you."

Delicate was a nice way of saying that the idiot in charge of the last mission to Andalyssia had been a moron who had somehow managed to upset an entire country. Jean-Paul didn't recall the precise details, as it had been some time ago, but he knew the Imperial army had been braced for rumblings of trouble from that part of the empire following the mission. They hadn't eventuated, but it had still taken months for the Andalyssians to agree to come to Lumia to meet with Aristides. It rarely took months for Aristides to get his way on a matter, which was proof of just how delicate the situation was. Aristides was buttering the Andalyssians up. Which made Jean-Paul's role crystal clear.

"You want the son of a duq to make them feel important." Jean-Paul rolled his eyes and didn't look at his father. Andre had campaigned with Aristides's father and had made a name for himself as something of a diplomat in his youth. He still acted as an advisor to the emperor on matters of some of the farther-flung parts of the empire at times. Usually those times involved Andre having a broader game in mind. Or just being in the mood to meddle. In this case, Jean-Paul hoped he wasn't trying to gain favor with Aristides in order to get the emperor to lean on Jean-Paul to be a good boy and marry.

"Precisely," Aristides said. "But don't worry, you will work with my guards. We just need you to play nice and make sure our friends from Andalyssia are happy. We will hold a welcome ball a few days after they arrive. That should placate them somewhat."

Jean-Paul hid his wince. He didn't mind balls like tonight's so much, the ones that were more social occasions for the court than anything. They, of course, came with politics and posturing, but not to the level seen at the more formal balls held when Aristides had a point to make or a message to deliver. Those were far more tedious, every move and word needing to be considered and analyzed. He had to pay attention to court politics. It was part of being who he was. That didn't mean he had to enjoy the worst aspects of it. But he did have to obey his emperor. "Of course, Your Imperial Majesty. I look forward to it."

Aristides's mouth quirked, but he didn't call Jean-Paul on the lie. Instead he turned to Andre and said, "There, my lord. Your son has accepted his task. Perhaps you would allow us to talk alone for a few moments? I hate to think I am keeping you from this evening's pleasantries."

The speed with which his father complied with this request made the hairs on the back of Jean-Paul's neck prickle. So he wasn't surprised when Aristides walked over to the sideboard, poured himself a glass of ilvsoir, and then settled into one of the delicate gilt chairs, gesturing for Jean-Paul to sit too before saying, "Danced with any pretty girls tonight?"

Now that they were alone, Jean-Paul didn't need to be polite. "What did my father promise you to get you to ask me that?" He lowered himself carefully onto a chair. Palace furniture tended toward spindly-legged styles that were not designed for someone of his size. Though these were more comfortable than some of the torture devices disguised as furniture Aristides used in some of the audience chambers he reserved for people he didn't want to encourage to linger.

Aristides grinned. "Can't I be concerned over my friend's lonely bachelorhood?"

"Given it hasn't much concerned you before now, no. I'm in no hurry to follow you into matrimony. Unlike you, I don't have an empire to secure with heirs." Aristides had married young. He and his empress had produced a crown prince and three princesses since then. Their children were spread out over twelve years. Alain was just eighteen. Cecilie, the youngest, was six. And the empress was unexpectedly—to the court, at least—pregnant again. Perhaps that was what was making Aristides family minded.

"A duq also has a line to secure," Aristides retorted.

"I'm not duq yet," Jean-Paul said. "And I have siblings. Nothing's going to happen to the San Pierre legacy if something happens to me."

"I prefer you to your siblings."

"Well, my younger brother is a twit, I grant you that. The girls are both sensible, though."

"There has never, to my knowledge, been a Duquesse of San Pierre in her own right," Aristides said. "I have enough trouble with things at the moment without your family causing an uproar by failing to pass the title to a male heir."

"Then you'll take the twit and set my sisters to managing him. They'll find him a sensible wife," Jean-Paul said, then realized he had perhaps made a tactical error in reintroducing the subject of marriage.

Aristides smiled, the expression edged. "I'd rather find you a sensible wife. Your father mentioned Celadin?"

"Celly would rather eat her entire collection of shoes than marry me, I expect." Jean-Paul waved a dismissive hand. He'd known Celadin de Bretani since they'd both been small. Never had the slightest desire to kiss her, nor, as far as he could tell, she him. "We get along, but nothing more than that."

"Your father reliably informs me that the breeding of heirs doesn't require such things." Aristides smirked and drank again.

"Says the man who adores his wife." True, Aristides hadn't had much time to choose when he'd been pressed to marry so young, but in Liane, he had made a match with someone he could love.

"I'm perfectly prepared to let you marry someone you adore, too," Aristides said. He tapped his glass with one long brown finger, dark eyes serious. "But you need to find her. Your father, I suspect, will start to force the issue if you do not take some action soon. So consider this my hint to start to take action."

Jean-Paul thought of Imogene and the action he would have been taking with her right now if he hadn't been interrupted. He frowned, wondering if she would indeed be waiting for him when he returned. His frown turned to a grin that he had to work to regulate to something less enthusiastic.

Aristides cleared his throat. "Am I to take it from your expression that there may be a candidate?"

"For marriage? No." The lieutenant was beautiful, but they had only just met. He wasn't going to confuse attraction for affection so soon.

"Ah. So we interrupted something more...temporary? In which case, my friend, I shall consider my duty to your father done and release you back to your entertainments, such as they are. Major Perrine will be in touch with you tomorrow about the Andalyssians."

"I look forward to it," Jean-Paul lied again.

Major Perrine, the second-in-command of Aristides's personal guard, was a good man but somewhat of a stickler for detail. A good quality in someone in charge of the emperor's safety. Less good if he was to be in charge of Jean-Paul, too. Technically they shared a rank. But it was Jean-Paul being inserted into the guards' usual sphere of operations, and Perrine's rank was somewhat less newly minted than Jean-Paul's own. Which meant he had to follow Perrine's orders. "Are you returning to the ball?"

"Not just yet," Aristides said. "I have other conversations to hold." He looked down at his glass as though resenting the fact. He wore the weight of his crown lightly most of the time, but there were moments when Jean-Paul glimpsed the price he paid for his power.

"Then I will bid you good night, Your Imperial Majesty."

"And I will bid you good hunting, my friend."

Chapter Nine

❧❀❧

The last person Imogene expected to see coming around the corner of the main barracks of the Imperial Mage Corps two days after the ball was the vanishing son of a duq himself.

Dressed in imperial black, brows drawn down as though contemplating something unpleasant, he didn't look as though he was expecting to see her either. But when he did, his face broke into a smile that chased away the regret she'd been trying to ignore since their evening had ended so abruptly. A sensation that was both pleasant and somewhat...alarming.

"Lieutenant," he said. "This is an unexpected pleasure."

"Major du Laq." She saluted—they were, after all, both in uniform—wrestling her expression away from the tickle in her cheek muscles that wanted to smile right back at him.

The sight of him instantly lifted her mood, but she didn't want to let him know that just yet. Not after he'd failed to reappear at the ball.

She'd waited for him for almost an hour, lingering around the edge of the dance floor, pretending to sip more campenois and watch the dancers while fending off offers from other men.

But as the time had stretched, she'd begun to think perhaps he wasn't returning. Then Chloe had found her, armed with an invitation to continue on to a smaller gathering.

She could hardly refuse to go. Friendship trumped new flirtations. Besides, she'd had no idea whether her flirtation was coming back. A fact her body had lamented even as she'd left with Chloe and her friends.

"So formal, Lieutenant," Jean-Paul said. "Does this mean your disappearance from the ball indicated a sudden change of...heart?"

Imogene glanced around. They weren't inside the barracks, but this wasn't a conversation she would be keen for her fellow mages to overhear. By a strict reading of the rules, there was no issue with an officer in the mages being involved with one from the regulars, but it wasn't encouraged. Not that she was planning on being involved with the man, but his rank was an added complication. One she'd forgotten to consider back there in the ballroom with his hands on her waist and those storm cloud eyes making it hard to think.

They were making it hard to think now. The man was no less handsome out of his evening clothes. Perhaps even more so. The sleek lines of the uniform suited him better than the frippery of court dress. But no, she had to think not of how good he looked but whether she still wanted to encourage him at all.

"I'm not entirely sure this is the time and place for such a conversation, Major," she said. "I have to report for duty."

Not duty exactly. Generally officers were granted a week's leave following an extended foreign mission unless the army had urgent need of their services. She'd submitted all her reports, so her time was her own. But Colonel Ferritine had sent a note to request her to come to headquarters. Given he was the one who would decide whether she would be allowed to bond a sanctii, she wasn't going to keep him waiting.

"Is Colonel Ferritine your commander?" Jean-Paul said. "I'll walk with you. I have an appointment with Major Perrine."

He did? She felt her brows rise. The cavalry didn't usually cross paths with the Imperial Guard unless the emperor was going somewhere beyond the city. The guard protected their turf zealously when it came to asserting authority over the emperor's safety. But a lieutenant didn't ask a major why he was meeting with another senior officer.

"Very well."

"But before we go, Lieutenant, I wondered if you might like to try dancing with me again? There is another ball at the palace in three days' time. It would be my pleasure to secure you an invitation. If you haven't had that change of heart I mentioned earlier?"

That was clear enough. He was interested enough to pursue the matter further. Though she wasn't sure how clear to be in return. Or if it was the wisest move to accept his invitation. The man was handsome, and his touch had made her breathless, but her career was at a delicate point. But surely just one night couldn't hurt. She could even bring Chloe to lend respectability to her appearance at another ball. "Just me?"

He frowned. "Is there someone else you would like to bring?"

"My friend, Chloe Matin," she said quickly, wondering why she was so keen to correct any misapprehension of his that she might have a man in mind.

"The Maistre's daughter?" His expression eased, and he nodded. "That would present no problem.

Though is she likely to take it amiss if I monopo-
lize your time?"

She smiled up at him. Chloe had managed herself well enough at the ball. She had known more
people there than Imogene, in fact. "I'm sure she
will not."

His smile matched her own. "Then, Lieutenant,
I will have an invitation delivered to you. Now, let
us walk. I wouldn't want to make you late."

Imogene's mind was still half on Jean-Paul as she
walked into Colonel Ferritine's office. Which was
why, perhaps, she came to a less than graceful halt
when she registered that both Major Fontaine and
Captain Brodier were in the room. She gathered
her wits long enough to snap a salute. Honore
flashed her a quick encouraging smile before her
expression turned back to a more professional
calm one.

"Don't look so alarmed, Lieutenant," Colonel
Ferritine said. He gestured to the plain wooden
chair beside Honore. "Take a seat." The colonel
had short gray hair and lines in his face that spoke
of his years of experience. His bright blue eyes
looked friendly rather than annoyed, so Imogene
hoped that was a good sign and she wasn't about to
be hauled over the coals by all three of her commanding officers. Not that she could think of anything she might have done that would warrant it.
Attending a ball wasn't forbidden. Still, she settled
herself fast and stayed silent, waiting to find out
why she was there.

"I believe you spoke to Captain Brodier about
sanctii the other day," Colonel Ferritine said. "Have
you thought more on what you discussed?"

"I have," Imogene said, keeping her voice

steady. She folded her hands in her lap as her pulse sped up a little. "I know it's not a decision to be taken lightly, but it is something I am interested in pursuing, if it would help my work." There. That sounded like she was being a good little soldier rather than one enticed by the idea of having a sanctii for more selfish reasons.

The three officers exchanged a look. Imogene clasped her hands tighter, unsure what that might mean.

"It is not a choice you can make lightly," the colonel agreed. "But at this moment, there may be a case for making it quickly."

"Sir?" Imogene said, hoping she sounded enthusiastic rather than entirely unsure what the colonel was talking about.

"Our next round of preparatory training for those wishing to attempt a bond starts next week. As you know, we consider and select our candidates with great care. The decisions are made well in advance. But, as it happens, one of our candidates has changed his mind and does not wish to undertake the training."

Imogene racked her brain, trying to think who it might be. The process by which the army chose mages for this was secretive, as was the training that followed. The candidates held things close to their chest until they either succeeded or failed in their attempts. And those who failed sometimes pretended they hadn't even tried. Failure wasn't seen as a black mark on your career—bonding a sanctii was difficult and required a great deal of power—but Imogene imagined it could only feel like a catastrophe to try but fail. There were often whispers of speculation about who might be chosen, but she'd been out of the country for months now. She'd lost track of who could be in the running. But equally, she'd heard nothing of any junior officers being injured or ill. She couldn't imagine what else would make someone give up the chance.

"So, we have a slot to fill, Lieutenant." Colonel Ferritine nodded at her and then at Major Fontaine. "The major tells me Cesarus speaks favorably of you."

He did? That startled her enough that she turned her head to look at Major Fontaine. Who merely smoothed his neatly trimmed red beard and gestured her back to the colonel.

"All other reports are favorable, too. You have been an exemplary young officer since your first mission. And, on short notice, we don't have another candidate more suitable to put forward."

"You want me to bond a sanctii now?" It came out squeakier than she'd intended.

The colonel grinned. "Not right this minute. But soon. I understand, Lieutenant, that this requires some consideration on your part. But we need to know by the end of the week. If you accept this offer, you would commence training next week. If you say no now, it will not reflect badly on you, but I cannot promise you a place in the next round or even tell you when the next training might occur. You know how long the training lasts? And that you are confined to the training barracks while undertaking your studies?"

She nodded. Ten days for the initial training, she knew. Which covered more on sanctii lore and the learning of the very precise details of the bonding itself. After that, individual mages could take longer to study and prepare themselves. Mages outside the army sometimes took months. But she wouldn't have months. A mage who didn't have the courage to make an attempt as soon as possible would be quietly discouraged from trying at all. And that would be a bigger failure than failing to form the bond at first attempt.

A shiver ran down her spine. There was a healthy dose of apprehension now mingled with excitement. This was serious business. A decision that would change her life. Very few mages released a sanctii from its bond once they had one. If she chose to do this, she would have a sanctii watching her, helping her, linked to her until she died. A bond more intimate than marriage in a way. But the fact that there was still excitement mingled with the fear told her that she still wanted to try.

"You need my decision by the end of the week?" she asked, pleased that she sounded calm and direct.

"Yes. You have until then. Sooner would be better. It would give you more time to prepare yourself. I know you are on leave after your mission and were probably minded to pursue some frivolity, but this choice requires care. I trust your judgment, Lieutenant. I know you will take time to consider before you make it. But you should consider quickly. A good officer knows when to be bold, after all."

Chapter Ten

***

"What do you think is keeping him?" Chloe whispered to Imogene as they surveyed the ballroom at the palace.

The assembled nobles were mingling and talking, waiting for the emperor to make his appearance and formally open the ball. But he was late now, late enough that the buzz of conversation had turned from congenial to a more speculative note.

Imogene twitched her skirt out of the path of a young aristo walking past her with no regard for anyone in his immediate surroundings. "Your guess is as good as mine at this point." She tried to sound as though she didn't much care. But as Jean-Paul had not yet appeared either—making her think, given his visit to Major Perrine, that perhaps his role tonight was more than just courtier—she *did* care.

She'd been looking forward to tonight. Frankly, between the nerves as she tried to determine for sure that she wanted to bond a sanctii and the anticipation of seeing Jean-Paul again and discovering what may happen if they were not interrupted once more, there had been enough adrenaline running through her system for the last three days that she needed to do something to burn it off and clear her head. She was rather hoping the something would be Jean-Paul, but that did require the man to actually appear.

But before she could grow too anxious, the buzz of voices quieted and the ball-goers began to turn, as though pulled by a hidden thread, toward the far end of the ballroom where the emperor held court. Imogene and Chloe, being relatively unimportant, were nowhere close enough to see much more than the backs of other people's heads. Chloe, who was taller, stood on her tiptoes, craning her neck in a way that was not strictly ladylike.

"Can you see anything?" Imogene asked.

"The emperor, I think," Chloe said. "And the empress." She teetered for a moment, and Imogene put a hand on her arm to steady her. "Major Perrine. And...I'm not sure. Is there a delegation expected? There are several people wearing long robes. All embroidered and pleated. I don't recognize the style."

Imogene stiffened. Long pleated and embroidered robes? That sounded painfully familiar. "What colors?" she hissed.

"Shades of green and a very peculiar orange. I'm not sure it's the best combination." Chloe glanced sideways at Imogene with a smirk. "Your mother's clothier would not approve."

Imogene smoothed a hand down the skirt of her own crimson dress, trying to smooth away the nerves suddenly gripping her stomach. Orange and green embroidered robes. Court robes from *Andalyssia*. Their particular style of intricate geometric embroidery was burned deep in her brain. Beautiful, in its own way, but unfortunately also too wrapped up in the memories of her disastrous first assignment. All those disapproving pale-skinned faces glaring above the robes as the senior of the king's Ashmeiser—had made it clear that the Illvyan diplomats would be best to return to Lumia. Technically he hadn't had the authority to expel Illvyans, but at that stage even Captain Berain had realized the mission was an unredeemable failure and there had been little point remaining.

"Andalyssians," she said, the words half breath.

Chloe's head snapped back round. "Andalyssians? Wasn't that where—"

"Yes," Imogene said, stomach churning with the sudden need to leave. "I'm not sure I should be here. If the emperor is hosting a delegation from Andalyssia, he must be trying to mend fences. I doubt he wants anyone from that mission present."

She tried to keep a scowl off her face. Goddess curse it. Had Jean-Paul known about this when he'd invited her? And if he had, did that mean he didn't know she was one of the junior officers on that mission? Granted, he was in the cavalry, not the mages, but the army was the army, and the speed at which gossip and bad news traveled was faster than anything other than perhaps a sanctii. She'd suffered through weeks of pitying looks anywhere she'd gone within the barracks before she'd been sent off to the first of her courier jobs to start earning back some trust. She'd gritted her teeth—after all, she had done nothing wrong on the mission—and kept her nose clean and lived it down. Or so she thought. But if any of the Andalyssians recognized her here tonight, goddess only knew how they might take it. "I should go."

"You can't leave now," Chloe hissed back. "That will only draw more attention."

She had a point. No one in the ballroom was moving, all eyes turned attentively toward the emperor. If Imogene tried to retreat now, it would cause a commotion. And possibly draw the focus of one of the Imperial Guard.

"Fine." She gritted her teeth and tried to look

as though she was paying attention as the emperor
began to speak. His voice, enhanced by magic, carried over the crowd. Imogene only half paid attention, her mind racing, trying to think of the fastest
way to get out of the ballroom once the emperor
finished his speech. Anxiety twisted with disap-
pointment in her stomach. It seemed she and Jean-
Paul would be thwarted again. Maybe that was just
as well.

The Andalyssians' presence was a sharp reminder that she couldn't afford any hint of scandal
right now. And no matter how temporary a night in
Jean-Paul's bed might seem, it would only take a
slip of the tongue on his part or for someone to see
them and put two and two together for the rumors
to spread.

The emperor's words continued rolling over the
crowd. The diplomat in Imogene translated the
tone of polite phrases as conciliatory, but also a
little impatient. The emperor wanted to get the
relationship with Andalyssia back to stable ground,
and quickly.

But even the analysis of the meaning beneath
the message didn't distract her from her desire to
leave. Nor did the emperor do anything that might
have eased her concerns by naming the Andalyssians. That much at least would have told her
if there was anyone amongst them who might recognize her. She'd been very junior in the mission,
but she'd spent time at the Andalyssian court and
in the meetings that went along with any mission.

True, she'd always been seated in the rear of the
room, bent over a sheaf of papers, taking notes, or
running messages. They'd only been in the country
two weeks before they'd been asked to leave. Long
enough for her to have grown familiar with all the
immediate members of the court they'd had deal-
ings with in their talks, and quite a few more who'd

been present at the social gatherings she'd attended.

Most Andalyssians were pale and blonde and green eyed. They had female mages, but the unusual kind of earth magic they practiced seemed to tint their hair more copper than the deep scarlet that streaked through Imogene's natural dark brown. She'd been noticeable at the Andalyssian court even when trying to fade into the background. And surely the Andalyssians would have sent experienced courtiers to Lumia. Exactly the sort most likely to remember her.

By the time the emperor finished and the court broke once more into conversation as the music began, she was desperate to leave. She took Chloe's hand and tugged her toward the nearest door.

"Is this really necessary?" Chloe protested, though she was well schooled enough to do so with a smile pasted on her face.

"I'm sorry," Imogene said. "I know you were looking forward to this." She didn't slow her pace.

"What about your mystery man?" Chloe said. "I thought you wanted to meet up with him?"

Chloe had somehow missed Jean-Paul's dance with Imogene at the first ball, being too caught up with her group of friends, and so had no idea who had secured their invitation for tonight. Imogene hadn't told her anything more than she'd met someone perhaps worthy of a dalliance. It had seemed safer. Chloe would only get overinvested if she realized who Jean-Paul was, and there was nothing to get invested in.

"I think the goddess is sending me a sign that he and I are perhaps not a good idea." Imogene tried to sound less disappointed than she felt. A large part of her body thrummed with annoyance and frustration, even though her brain so far had kept control and remembered the sensible reasons why she needed to leave the palace before she could cause any problems for the emperor.

Chloe made a dissatisfied noise that suggested she thought the goddess was a spoilsport, but she followed Imogene without further protest.

Until they pushed through one of the side doors near the rear of the room, made it about twelve feet down the corridor outside, and nearly barreled into Jean-Paul striding in the other direction.

Chapter Eleven

※❧❀❧※

"Lieutenant," he said with an unmistakable thrum of pleasure in his voice as they righted themselves and regrouped in such a way that Chloe stood next to Jean-Paul facing Imogene. "We have to stop meeting this way."

Chloe's brows flew upward.

"Major," Imogene replied, avoiding using his name. "We were just leaving."

"So soon?" His expression fell. "But the dancing has only just begun. And you and—Mamsille Matin, is it not—are far too beautiful tonight to go before you grant some of us men the pleasure of your company on the dance floor."

He turned toward Chloe and bowed shallowly. "Mamsille Matin, I will introduce myself, as the lieutenant seems to have neglected to do so. Major Jean-Paul du Laq, at your service."

Chloe's brows flew higher, and she mouthed, "du Laq?" at Imogene before schooling her face back to a polite smile as Jean-Paul straightened. "A pleasure, Major du Laq."

Jean-Paul smiled at her, but then his attention arrowed back to Imogene. "Can I not persuade you to stay, Lieutenant?"

Chloe smirked at Imogene. Clearly her friend

had made the connection that Jean-Paul was Imogene's mystery man. And worse, it was obvious that
Chloe knew who he was.

Now she would never hear the end of it. Even if
they left right now, Chloe wouldn't let Imogene get
away with avoiding the subject of why the son of a
duq was interested in her. Worse, the uncomfortable truth was that Imogene, faced with Jean-Paul
again, didn't want to get away.

But as much as she wanted nothing more than
to let Jean-Paul take her hand and lead her where
he would because, really, she kept forgetting just
how handsome he was, she maintained a semblance
of control. "I'm afraid not. Circumstances have altered, it seems."

"Circumstances?" He looked confused. "Do you
have a more pressing engagement elsewhere?"

"No, she doesn't," Chloe said cheerfully, grin
widening.

"I do," Imogene insisted. "Chloe is just trying
to be polite, Major, but we really must go." She narrowed her eyes at Chloe.

Jean-Paul's eyes narrowed, too. "I do not wish
to keep you, Lieutenant, but I would appreciate it
if you would grant me a minute of your time first.
Alone," he added.

"I don't—"

"Think of it less as a request and more as an
instruction from a superior officer," he said, voice
rumbling through her.

There was no way to refuse that. He outranked
her. "Sir," she said stiffly.

"I'll go arrange for our carriage to be summoned," Chloe said, making it clear that she was
not going to come to Imogene's rescue. She hurried
away down the corridor, leaving Imogene with
Jean-Paul.

"Well?" she said. "Do you have any more orders for me, Major?"

He rolled his eyes. "Don't be dramatic." He jerked his head toward a door a few feet behind her. "We can talk in there."

She should say no and go after Chloe, and then this mad temptation would be done with. But he did outrank her and could cause problems if she ignored him. Of course, if he was the kind of man who would cause her problems over this, then she was well rid of him.

But despite all of that, she wasn't ready to step away from her fascination. So she followed him into the room and let him close the door behind them. It was one of the many rooms used by the court for meetings and business and politicking in the polite-on-the-surface aristo fashion. Furnished with a table just big enough for the four chairs tucked against its edges, plus a small sofa and pair of armchairs closer to the fireplace. Which was lit despite the unlikeli-hood of anyone seeking to use this room tonight.

She moved toward the flickering light of the flames, sending power into the earth-lights as well. The room brightened.

Good. Better for them not to be alone in the dark just now.

Jean-Paul followed her over to the fire, standing silent beside her.

Imogene resisted the urge to step closer as she took in his scent. "You wanted to talk to me, sir?"

He winced. "I apologize for pulling rank. That was wrong of me. But I didn't want you to leave. Not without knowing why."

She hesitated. He sounded sincere enough, but this felt like more than she had bargained for. Ex-planations and misunderstandings, and they hadn't yet so much as kissed. For a brief liaison, it was rapidly growing complicated. A wise woman would make an excuse and then hurry to find Chloe as fast as she could. But she was discovering that, when it came to this man, perhaps she wasn't so wise. So perhaps she should just be honest. It was simplest in the end.

"It isn't you. It's the Andalyssians."

He looked confused. "Why should a group of foreign northerners with their noses out of joint upset you? Granted, their fashion is somewhat eye-watering, but..." He raised an eyebrow at her, inviting her to fill him in.

"Because I was part of that mission to Andalyssia that went...wrong. The reason their northern noses are out of joint, as you say," she said, bracing herself for his reaction. "You didn't know that?"

He frowned, head tilting. "No. Why should I?"

"Because everybody knows about that mission," she said. Because it had taken her this long to overcome the blot on her record and earn another chance. But maybe the son of a duq didn't know much about having to fight for each step forward in a career. Or having to overcome setbacks. She doubted he'd faced many of those.

Jean-Paul shrugged. "I'm cavalry. You didn't cause a war, so we don't get involved." He held up a large hand. "I knew something had gone wrong and that Alexei Berain resigned, but I never heard the details or any gossip about the junior officers."

Making him one of the few people in the army who hadn't.

"Well, there was plenty of gossip. And plenty of recriminations to go around. So I don't think it's a good idea if they see me at the emperor's ball."

"Why, Lieutenant, that sounds like you're running from a fight."

"I'm a diplomat. I'm supposed to avoid fights. In fact, that's my entire job."

"Not exactly. It's more that you're supposed to win the fight without getting blood on the ground. Or the carpet, I suppose." He grinned down at her. "I promise you there will be no bloodshed in the ballroom. Major Perrine has the place crawling with his men."

"And doesn't that tell you the situation is precarious?"

"Perrine is cautious. It's his job. But he didn't strike me as a man on high alert. Well, no more than he usually does. Given I've spent half my time with him the last few days, I would hope he would have told me if he was expecting any real trouble."

"If he's not expecting trouble, then why are the cavalry involved?" Imogene asked.

Chapter Twelve

Jean-Paul pulled a face. "Not so much the cavalry as just me. And I'm mostly being decorative."

He certainly glittered in his black dress uniform, with medals and ribbons of honor arrayed across the impressive expanse of his chest. Some were marks of his regiment and rank, but others were from actual fighting. He hadn't just stayed safely in the capital, it seemed. "Decorative? Did the emperor think his ballroom would lack for handsome men tonight?"

His smile grew wider, his expression delighted. "Handsome, am I?"

She shook her head. "Some might think so. Those who weren't waiting for an answer to their question."

He laughed. "A point, Lieutenant. Very well. No, not that kind of decorative. Even if Aristides was inclined to admire men's faces, not women's, I doubt I would be high on his list. No, my value comes in my rank. If dealing with disgruntled diplomats from the outer reaches of the empire, it can be useful to have the son of a duq or someone equally impressive-sounding to dance attendance on them. Make them feel important."

She understood that much. "I see. But if that's your role here tonight, then shouldn't you already be at the ball doing whatever it is dancing attendance involves? Not consorting in dimly lit rooms with women who would probably not please said disgruntled diplomats."

"Consorting? That hardly seems a fair assessment, Lieutenant. We've barely touched." He brushed his hand over hers, then pulled it back.

For a moment she forgot what the point of their conversation was. Something about...Andalyssians. Right. Bloody inconvenient Andalyssians. Because if not for them, his hand could be doing more than just wafting over her fingers right now.

"Let's not argue about terminology. You should be back in there"—she jerked her head in the direction of the ballroom—"doing what you're here for today." She tapped a finger on the biggest and the brightest of the medals on his chest. An imperial commendation, she thought it was, though she had never seen one up close. A golden star with a spray of tiny sapphires embedded in each point. "You're in uniform. You have a job to do." She peered up at him. "And you must have known that when you invited me here tonight. So how exactly were you expecting this evening to go, Major?"

"I'm on duty, but I'm not part of the guard itself. My job is to mingle and ensure that the Andalyssians meet the right members of the court. The ones who will make them feel valued. I was reliably informed that they will retire early, and then my time will be my own. Or all yours, Lieutenant." His gaze skimmed over her body. "And seeing you in that dress, I must tell you I am very tempted to go fetch a sleeping draught of some sort and pour it into their damned campenois to hurry their departure along."

"I'm not sure drugging a delegation is the way to repair relations." She tried to pretend she couldn't feel the weight of his gaze on her skin like the heat from the flames. Her skin prickled with the need to move closer to him.

"Andalyssia can rot for all I care right now," he said. He reached out a hand, settled it on her waist. "Stay."

"That wouldn't be helpful." It would be everything every inch of her body wanted, but not helpful to anything but her worse instincts. "This can only be a fleeting thing, you and me. It's not worth a diplomatic incident." But she made no move to shift his hand from her waist. Instead she stepped closer, unthinking as his fingers tugged her toward him.

"Fuck diplomacy," he growled and bent his mouth to hers.

And oh, his mouth.

She'd never had a man deploy a kiss like a weapon before, but his found her like an arrow flying true and shattered her defenses.

One taste of him and her common sense dissolved under a rush of lightning-hot want. It was like the first time she'd touched a ley line, back when her powers had manifested. A sense of the world being forever changed as power and emotion surged through her. A sense of wanting nothing more than to remain suspended in the sensation forever. If he'd been an illusioner, she would have suspected him of using magic to sway her senses, but she felt nothing magical flaring from him as he poured his kiss into her, only desire that was as intoxicating as any touch of magic she'd known.

She swayed into him, opening her lips and kissing him back just as fiercely. Let herself take what he was offering and offer something of her own in return. Lost in the moment and the touch of him. Until he pulled back, staring down at her with eyes that were black now, his pupils blown wide with only the faintest rim of gray around them. There was no mistaking how much he wanted her. His lips had left hers, but his hands still held her fast against him, and even through the layers of ball gown and petticoats, she could feel him pressing into her.

"Stay," he muttered again. "Please, Imogene."

Goddess. The way he said her name. She could cope with his teasing "Lieutenant," but not with him speaking the three syllables of her name like they were half a prayer. Her blood was roaring in her ears, her pulse still pounding from his kiss, and she couldn't have moved away from him in that moment if the emperor himself had appeared and demanded it.

"I don't want to cause trouble. And I can't afford another blot on my record." Her invitation to bond a sanctii could vanish as swiftly as it had been extended.

He shook his head. "If there was any concern over you attending this ball, Major Perrine would have told me. He vets the invitation list thoroughly."

Of course he had. She felt foolish. In her surprise, she hadn't stopped to think that, of course, the emperor knew each guest who attended his balls. And she had been approved. Relief swept over her. Followed by a second rush of nerves. Not caused by the Andalyssians but by the awareness that if she did stay, if she went back to the ballroom with Jean-Paul, then... She stared up at him, wondering again if it was a mistake to give in to wanting him.

"Stay, Imogene. I will get the damned Andalyssians out of the ballroom as soon as I can. Then I will find you and we will dance. And then, unless you tell me no, I will take you back to my apartment and remove that delectable dress and we will finish what we just started."

It was just as well that he was still holding her because her knees wobbled a little at the words. Which was ridiculous. She wasn't a woman whose knees wobbled because a man announced that he wanted her. She hadn't been that way even when she'd been a virgin. She'd chosen her first lover—and every one since—with care and deliberation. She'd enjoyed herself. She'd learned what pleased her and what pleased them, but she had never been at risk of coming undone from just a kiss. Never been more certain that she should walk away before he could do anything more. Never been more certain that she had no intention of doing so.

"I'll stay," she said. "I'll wait for you."

"And then?" he asked, voice half a growl.

"And then, Major, we will...dance."

Chapter Thirteen

She was growing convinced that someone was manipulating with time in the ballroom. Jean-Paul had said he would try to get the Andalyssians to leave as soon as possible, but two hours had passed since she and Chloe had returned to the ballroom, and the Andalyssians showed no sign of leaving yet. She'd tried to stay inconspicuous, lingering near the edges of the room farthest from the emperor's party, but she'd had to accept several invitations to dance. Her nerves had eased somewhat after the first time she'd been whirled past the end of the room where the emperor and most of the Andalyssians were seated. None of them had so much as blinked at her, reducing her fear that one of them would recognize her and demand that she be removed from the palace. But she still didn't want to chance a close encounter.

On the third or fourth dance, she'd briefly caught Jean-Paul's eye from where he stood talking with the emperor, and he'd offered a quick smile and a small shrug of apology before she'd whirled on. The Andalyssians had started to join in some of the dances, and she thought someone had been giving them lessons, as they seemed adept at the fast-paced waltzes and gigues, which were different to the slow elaborate patterns of the set dances she'd seen in their country.

Still, their participation in the dances had made her think it wiser to decline the next offer she'd had from a dance partner and to go instead to find Chloe.

She made her way down the far side of the ballroom where there were thoughtfully placed niches curtained in gold-worked satin to allow the courtiers to retire in small groups or twosomes for more private discussions or entertainments. Probably the latter. Anyone who wanted to discuss anything truly private would be taking a risk. They could, of course, use a ward, but using magic in the emperor's presence was not encouraged.

Of course, they risked being overheard if they chose to undertake a liaison of a more intimate nature in one of the niches as well, but that didn't seem to be of as much concern judging by the sounds coming from the first two she passed.

The third was empty, as was the fourth. She paused there, taking a moment to enjoy the spectacle of the dancers swirling past. But her attention was dragged back when an oddly familiar voice caught her ear.

Not speaking Illvyan. No, the words were Andalyssian. The sounds of it were unmistakable. She'd studied the language before her mission there. She'd not reached any great degree of fluency, but she knew its rhythms. The peculiar combination of sharp consonants and hissing sibilants that made it stand out from the more liquid rhythm of Illvyan.

And the voices were coming from the fifth niche. Its curtains were closed, a signal that those within were not to be disturbed. But what were Andalyssians doing in a secret conversation in the middle of the ball?

It seemed an odd choice. One that sent a prickle of alarm down her spine.

Unable to stop herself, she ducked back into the alcove next to the Andalyssians, pulling the curtains fast behind her.

The voices next door paused as though those within had maybe heard her. She froze, hoping she hadn't scared them off. Apparently she hadn't. The quiet conversation started up again. Definitely Andalyssian. But it seemed after months of not using the language, much of the vocabulary she'd known had faded from her memory. She couldn't understand much. Whoever it was—she wasn't sure if there were three or four separate voices—they were speaking in low tones. One, who spoke least but with the most assured cadence, was, she thought, the voice that had caught her attention. Familiar, but she couldn't quite put a face to the voice when it wasn't clear.

She'd only recognized two of the Andalyssians she'd seen so far, both men she remembered being as junior as she had been at the time she'd met them. It wasn't either one of them speaking. But Andalyssians tended to run to tall and blond, the men wore their hair in very similar braided lengths, and they were all wearing the orange and green of the royal house's robes rather than those that might indicate any personal rank so it was difficult to distinguish them at a distance. She hadn't yet seen all their faces, so she didn't know if there were others amongst the party who she had met.

And strain her ears as she might, the muffled words were hard to distinguish. She heard the name Deephilm, the Andalyssian capital, and several references to time and what she thought might be "waiting," or maybe that was "patience." It was one of those tricky tongues where sometimes only a slight twist of emphasis altered the meaning of words that otherwise sounded the same.

She pressed as close to the wall between the alcoves as she dared, but nothing else in the soft phrases came clear in her mind, making her wish once more for a sanctii. Or that she'd been offered the option of learning Andalyssian with the assistance of a sanctii's magic via a reveilé. But the army preferred its junior officers to learn languages the old-fashioned way, except in times of extreme need. The theory being that then, when they were more senior and perhaps in need of the level of fluency a reveilé could grant, they would have the basic understanding and vocabulary that made a reveilé more effective. Besides, her language tutors in the army had insisted you could learn much about a people and a country from the way their languages worked and that linguistics were another tool in a diplomat's arsenal. Language lessons came with history and politics and geography to underpin the words.

She remembered more of that than she did of the language itself, it seemed. Which left her only frustrated as the voices went silent. A swish of fabric, a low laugh, and the sound of footsteps were all she heard as the men left the niche. It was an effort not to follow immediately, but it would be difficult to explain what she had been doing lurking in a niche by herself. Unfortunately, by the time she deemed it safe to exit, there were no Andalyssians nearby at all, leaving her with nothing more than a vague sense that she'd missed something important for her pains.

Chapter Fourteen

"Bored with me already?" Jean-Paul murmured as he dipped Imogene into the next move of the dance. She was following him seamlessly, but her expression was distracted. Hardly the emotion he was trying to evoke.

Her gaze came back to him, and she made an apologetic face and then smiled. "Not bored, no."

They were moving closer to where the emperor still stood talking to the empress, who had made a late and somewhat unusual appearance at the ball. Liane was pregnant with their fifth child, and if the rumors he had heard over the years were true, her pregnancies had been difficult and there had been losses in between. Aristides's expression as he talked with his wife was tender. The Andalyssians had departed for bed twenty minutes or so ago, and Jean-Paul had excused himself from Aristides and gone in search of Imogene. Who now seemed more fascinated by the emperor than the dance.

"Perhaps if you tell me what is so distracting, we can solve the issue?" he said gently.

Her eyes whipped back to him again. "It's nothing."

"It's not nothing. Something is bothering you. If it's something I've done, I would prefer to know.

If it's something larger—which I am hoping it is given your attention returning to the emperor every time we get near him—then I would say it's my duty to know."

"No, I was just wondering how the Andalyssians enjoyed the ball."

"Ever the diplomat?" he said, one side of his mouth quirking. "You can be at ease, Lieutenant. No blood was shed. They appeared to enjoy themselves. Even the Ashmeiser Elannon, and he seems to have been born with no fraction of a sense of humor."

Imogene nearly stumbled, the movement the slightest pause before he steadied her.

She was flushed from the dance, but beneath the pink, he fancied her cheeks were paler than they had been before he had mentioned the Ashmeiser.

He tightened his grasp on her waist a fraction, wanting to let her know she was safe. "You know him, the Ashmeiser?"

"He was one of the king's advisors when we were in Andalyssia," she said. "I never liked him. And he definitely didn't seem to like Illvyans. I always wondered if..."

"If?" Jean-Paul prompted, steering them around a wayward couple who had careened somewhat out of the path of the dance. This particular waltz was complicated and fast, which was good because it would mean that everybody was too busy concentrating on the steps to pay attention to anyone else's conversation.

"If there was more to our mission going wrong than just Captain Berain being an idiot. I mean, it started well enough, but then things seemed to fall apart far too quickly and for reasons that never entirely made sense. I thought perhaps the Andalyssians—or some of them, at least, as the king himself was cordial in the beginning—were undermining us. If I were to choose the Andalyssian most likely to be doing so, the Ashmeiser would be high on the list."

Jean-Paul still wasn't certain what the Ashmeiser did. Andalyssians didn't have a noble class that operated in the same way as Illvya's. They had more elaborate family obligations and ties that balanced with rank. The Ashmeiser was head of one of those families. And some sort of senior counselor to the king. A man of power. Important enough to be sent to repair relations. But if Imogene's instincts were right—and he saw no reason she would dissemble about the mission when she had been honest with him so far—he was an interesting choice of man for the job.

"Did you tell anyone of your suspicions?" he asked.

"By the time I realized, things were already bad. I included my thoughts in my report when we returned, but I had no evidence of any wrongdoing. And Captain Berain had so thoroughly made a mess of it all that no one seemed to want to go digging for any other problems."

"The Ashmeiser has been polite enough, so far," Jean-Paul said. "Reminds me somewhat of a human icicle, but he hasn't done anything untoward."

"That's good." She chewed at her lip. "I think I heard him talking earlier. There was a group of Andalyssians talking in one of the niches." She nodded to the side of the ballroom. "I couldn't see who they were, but I knew one of the voices sounded familiar. I couldn't quite place the voice then, but I'm sure it was him."

"Did you catch anything of what they said?" Jean-Paul asked.

She shook her head, light sparking from the jewels in her ears. "My Andalyssian is very rusty.

I've had no need to use it in months. Plus, they were speaking softly. There was something about time and perhaps patience, but that was it. They mentioned the capital, Deephilm, several times. They sounded..." She hesitated. "Cautious," she said at last. "Or wary, perhaps." She frowned.

"Perhaps that's not unreasonable when they're in a strange country. Face-to-face with the emperor rather than dealing with diplomats in their own territory." Still, the Ashmeiser had not struck him as a man who was easily cowed. Was he bold enough to try something foolish?

"An emperor who perhaps some of them are not reconciled to?"

"Andalyssia has been part of the empire for nearly fifty years," Jean-Paul said. "It seems a little late to be staging a rebellion."

"Perhaps," Imogene said. "But men seem to have a strange fascination with land and power."

"And women don't?"

Her mouth quirked. "I'm sure some of them are obsessed, too. But I didn't notice any women in the Andalyssian party."

She was right about that. The Andalyssians had brought no women. Which was a point against them in his book. Either they were foolish in the attitudes to women and failed to understand the information women could access that men could not in a court or they were not willing to risk their women on what was supposed to be in a peaceful mission. But that was a worry for another time. He was tired of thinking about the Andalyssians. He wanted to focus on Imogene. "What about you?"

She shrugged, which was something of a feat given the position of her hands and arms. "I have no need for vast lands or vast wealth. Do I have dreams of a successful career? Yes. But that is not the same as conquest."

Jean-Paul wasn't so sure. He was beginning to feel somewhat as though she was conquering him. He took a deep breath, turning her again, and caught her scent. She wore a perfume that was unlike the heavy florals currently in fashion at court. Hers was greener, with a hint of spice and sweetness and a tang that reminded him of lemons. Had she bought it somewhere far away on her travels? Not that it mattered. He was near certain that she could wear no perfume at all and he'd still be fighting his every instinct that told him to pull her closer. To claim her.

He would take her to bed tonight. And tomorrow, well, as skittish as she seemed, he was hoping there might be something more to explore between them.

Her gaze had strayed again to the emperor.

"If it would ease your mind, I could mention to Aristides that the Andalyssians are whispering in corners."

Her eyes narrowed. "Are you making fun of me?"

"No, Lieutenant. You're the diplomat. I trust your instincts."

"Perhaps you should tell Major Perrine. He could set a watch."

"You mean set a sanctii?" he said. Sanctii could move invisible through a room. Part of what made them so valuable to the mages who had them. "You know that's not allowed when it comes to diplomats." Aristides had signed an agreement with the Andalyssians that set the terms of their visit. That included the provision of bags of salt to guard their rooms. He didn't know a lot about sanctii-he'd never shown any talent for water magic, so he had only received the basic knowledge of it that most Anglions did during his schooling, supplemented by somewhat more on the tactical use of the creatures during his service in the army—but he knew salt was their weakness. Too much of it hurt them and, more importantly, could snap the bond of magic between a sanctii and the mage controlling him. At best that meant the loss of a sanctii. At worst, it meant a dead mage if the sanctii had been displeased with his treatment while bonded. "But I can tell both the emperor and the major if that would set your mind at rest."

Chapter Fifteen

The smile that flashed over her face was lightning bright. He felt the weight of her delight in him like a physical blow that ignited a heat low in his belly. The musicians had reached the end passages of the dance. He didn't want to wait and linger through another.

"I will tell them now, after the dance. And then?" If he hadn't been dancing, he would have held his breath, waiting for her answer. He couldn't remember the last time a woman had him so hungry for her. Perhaps never.

The color had returned to her face, her cheeks flushed a shade that was a paler echo of the satin of her dress. Her lips were somewhere between the two colors, and imagining them darker and swollen from kisses did steal his breath.

"Then I believe you should call for your carriage, my lord. And take me somewhere we can be alone."

"As my lady wishes," he said and had never been so glad to hear the music come to an end. He escorted Imogene off the dance floor, told her sternly not to vanish anywhere, and headed for Aristides.

Unfortunately, he found his father first. The duq was standing with some of his friends—talking

politics, no doubt—but he broke away and beckoned to Jean-Paul when he spotted his son.

Jean-Paul gritted his teeth but obeyed the summons. His father would only bellow at him across
the room if he pretended not to have seen. He
bowed impatiently as his father studied him.

"In a hurry, Jean-Paul?" the duq asked.

"I want to speak to the emperor before I leave."

"It's early to be leaving." His father's eyes—the
same gray as his own—were cool.

"I've been with the Andalyssians all day. And I
will be again tomorrow. I think I've done my duty
for the day."

"If you'd done your duty, you would have been
dancing with Celadin or one of her friends."

Jean-Paul had caught sight of Celadin during
one of his waltzes with Imogene. She'd nodded ap-
provingly in his direction, then turned rapt attention back to her partner, the Marq de Illsien.

"I believe Celadin has plenty of partners to fill
her dance card."

"If you're not careful, she'll marry someone
else."

"And I'll be delighted to toast her at her wedding," Jean-Paul retorted. "Trust me, Father,
Celadin and I will never make a match."

"Then choose some other suitable girl. There
are plenty of them here tonight. You should be
dancing with them, not wasting your time on a
mere lieutenant with no name to speak of."

Goddess damn it. The duq had noticed. Worse,
he knew who Imogene was. A smart man would
dissemble. But when it came to Imogene, he clearly
wasn't that smart. But he *was* smart enough not to
let his father think he would succeed in choosing
Jean-Paul's wife for him.

Aristides had married at eighteen, when his father had fallen ill. He'd become a father for the

first time when he was still only eighteen, the need to do his duty to secure an heir for the empire more pressing than any personal preference. Jean-Paul had been ten when Aristides had wed, but he'd watched the emperor grow serious and stern near overnight, the hints of the younger man who'd seemed, despite their age difference, to be light-hearted and as eager to take part in whatever non-sense the boys of the court were getting up to buried under the weight of a crown and a family. Jean-Paul would do his duty, and he wanted sons and daughters of his own, yes, but he had promised himself that he would not be rushed or forced to the decision.

He had rarely been tempted to contemplate marriage before he had met Imogene. But he wanted to explore that temptation now. And he wouldn't let his father dissuade him.

"She's young. Who knows what she might become."

"I'm surprised Perrine let her in. She was part of the mission that is the reason we are here wining and dining those dull Andalyssians tonight."

He didn't take the bait and argue. That would only prolong the time away from Imogene. "Did you have something else you wanted from me, Father? Rather than telling me facts I already know and trying to arrange my life?"

His father's eyes narrowed. "It's my job to en-sure that the estate lies in safe hands."

Jean-Paul snorted. "Don't try that angle. At this point you need to either accept that you did your job in raising me to be a duq or throw me over for one of my brothers."

His father humphed. "I raised you to be smart. To see beyond the lure of a pretty face. Bed her if you must. But just remember where your true duty lies."

Chapter Sixteen

✢✢✢

Jean-Paul's apartment was not so much an apartment as a small jewel of a townhouse in Coteau-Arge, one of the wealthy areas of the city that shared a boundary with the palace grounds. Nowhere a mere major could afford to live. A reminder instead that he was a duq to be. Wealthy and powerful. And not hers. At least not after tonight.

He certainly hadn't wasted any time bundling her into a carriage once he had returned to the ballroom. There had been a certain tightness to his expression when he'd found her, but it eased when she had taken his arm to let him escort her away. The ball was still in full swing, and it was too early for the court to be leaving. But Jean-Paul didn't seem to care about that. As soon as the carriage had gotten well away from the lights of the palace forecourt and reached the dimly lit road that led through the grounds to the main gate, he'd lifted her onto his lap and kissed her again.

Which had driven all lingering doubts from her head. It was only the shortness of the journey that had meant they hadn't progressed much further than kissing. She'd never had sex in a carriage, and

Jean-Paul's was certainly large and luxurious enough that it would have been possible, but she wanted to savor him more if they were only to have one night.

They'd separated as the carriage had come to a halt, and the door to the townhouse had been opened by a manservant who had vanished when Jean-Paul told him he wouldn't need any more assistance for the night.

She had no idea if there were other servants. If there were, they didn't make themselves known.

And now she stood near shivering with wanting as she watched Jean-Paul pour them both a glass of campenois and wondering why he was wasting time with alcohol.

Still, she took the glass when he offered it and sipped politely. No doubt it was good—she hoped the son of a duq wouldn't serve bad wine—but her senses were too focused on him to spare the liquid bubbling over her tongue much effort. Jean-Paul rushing through her blood was headier than any wine she'd ever drunk.

Though she feared the aftermath may be as painful as the aftermath of an excess of alcohol.

But she'd set her feet upon this path, and no rational thought could stop her now.

Jean-Paul gestured at the wall, and the earth-lights there brightened.

She sent her magic searching down for a ley line. Of course there was one close to hand. A branch of the main line that ran below the palace. It answered her call, and power shimmered through her. She let go of the control of the sight and let herself see him with his magic. He didn't gleam bright as strong mages did. The light that shimmered over his skin, marking his power and his connection to the ley line, was subtler but somehow certain, as though rooted deep in the land. Solid. True. Earth magic and blood magic both, she thought. Which made sense for a warrior and a noble.

He would fight for what was his. And keep it close.

Well, she was never going to be his for long, but tonight she would savor him. She'd heard of strong powers that blended during sex and of mages using sex to deliberately combine their powers. She'd shared a bed with a strong mage or two in her time, but none of their kisses had ever made her feel like his.

Power wasn't what she wanted from him anyway. Tonight, she was more interested in passion.

She pushed the magic away, sending the lingering excess she'd pulled up from the line through the earth-lights, making them flare momentarily brighter. Careless of her. She knew how to shift power gracefully. But it seemed he had her off-balance.

Jean-Paul's brows lifted. "Did you like what you saw?"

Ah. She was discovered. He'd known she was looking at his magic. Had he sought hers as well? "Did you?"

"I don't need magic to like what I see when it comes to you, Lieutenant."

"Imogene," she corrected. She liked the way he used her rank. Teasing, yet respectful. But she wanted her name on his lips now. Wanted him to say it again, the way he'd said it when he'd first kissed her.

"As my lady wishes," he said. "Come here, Imogene."

That voice. It stroked her like rough silk. Commanding and enticing. She moved to him without thinking.

He took the glass from her hand, putting it and his aside. "What shall we do now, Imogene?" He brushed a curl back from her face.

She turned her head, nipped at his fingers. "I'm going to kiss you again. And then you're going to take me to bed."

"I like that plan."

"Good." She rose to her toes and put her hands around his neck, tugging his head down to hers. She wasn't short, but he was tall enough that she needed his cooperation if she was to avoid having to find a footstool to climb on to kiss him.

She smiled at the thought and he paused, his face close to hers.

"Something amusing?"

"I was just thinking of ways to get around you being so tall," she said.

His mouth curved, too. "Well, as to that. I find the best way is for you to get me to lie down."

"Do you respond to commands?" she asked.

"Sometimes," he said. "Sometimes I give them. Kiss me, Imogene. And we'll see who winds up on top."

"Is it a battle, then?" she breathed.

"A skirmish, perhaps," he said. "If we do it right."

A skirmish. She could handle that. A good way to think of it. A limited engagement. Not serious. And she would be the one to fire the opening shot. "Stop talking now," she said and kissed him.

As soon as his lips touched hers, she knew she was lost, though. Hopefully he would be, too. The best she could hope for was a draw, perhaps. Mutual satisfaction before they had to part. His mouth was warm and firm on hers, and she made a noise of pleasure.

That seemed to be all the encouragement he

needed. He lifted her as easily as she might lift a child and carried her through the darkened house, earth-lights flaring to light his way. She dimly registered the lights and the fact that they were moving upstairs, but as Jean-Paul apparently had a goddess-granted ability to walk, carry her, and kiss her at the same time, she paid little heed to anything but his mouth.

She made another murmuring sound of protest when he stopped kissing her to set her down at the foot of his bed, but given that letting go of her gave his hands freedom to roam over her body, she quickly became distracted again.

His fingers found the buttons at the back of her dress. "Buttons," he muttered. "Why do clothiers enjoy tiny buttons so much?"

She laughed. "Perhaps they wish to remind you men to take care when you have a woman's buttons to hand." Then she recalled the size of his hands and the size of the particular shimmery round buttons that graced this dress. It had taken Dina a few minutes to do them up, and she was well practiced with women's clothing.

"Do you need some assistance, my lord?" she asked.

"I can manage buttons," he muttered, but he did sound a little exasperated. "Or I have a pocketknife."

"This dress cost a small fortune," Imogene said. She clutched the bodice as it started to loosen. Obviously he had made some progress. "If you come at me with a knife, you'd best be prepared to defend yourself."

"Savage little thing, aren't you?"

"When it comes to defending the honor of my wardrobe, yes," she retorted. "I spend enough time in uniform that I appreciate wearing something pretty now and then."

"And I appreciate seeing you in something so lovely. But right now, I'm rather eager to see you out of it. Ah!" He made a pleased sound as his fingers stilled. "All done."

"Good." She let go of the bodice. The dress, with some small assistance from a wriggle of her hips, slid to the floor. Jean-Paul tugged at the ribbons that fastened the layers of petticoats to her waist, and they slid down to join the dress.

She took a breath, her heart pounding hard enough that she was somewhat surprised her corset strings didn't snap. But before she could worry too much about that, Jean-Paul's fingers skimmed down her back, and then he set to work on her corset as well. It took him less time than the buttons before he eased it apart, leaving her with only a shift and her underwear.

"So many layers," Jean-Paul murmured from behind her. "You are like a gift to be unwrapped, Imogene."

Right then, she felt more unraveled than unwrapped. As the heat of his hands grew more palpable with each layer of clothing he removed, she felt as though she might just melt down to become a puddle on the floor like her clothes.

She wanted him. Wanted him under her mouth, beneath her hands, wrapped around her. Wanted skin and sweat and sensation.

"I was never much good at unwrapping gifts," she said, turning to face him. "Too impatient. My mama used to call me greedy." She tugged her corset away from her body and shimmied it off. "Right now I'm greedy for you."

She'd never known that gray could be warm. But his eyes were, their depths inky and deep. His chest was rising and falling fast, too. It was still hidden from view beneath his shirt—he'd taken off his jacket when they'd arrived—but it seemed he was impatient, too.

She reached out and put her hand flat on his chest, seeking his heart. It might never be hers, but she would have the memory of it beating hard to her touch.

"Take me to bed, Jean-Paul."

Chapter Seventeen

He kissed her then. Wild and free and as greedy in his seeking of her as she was for him. Imogene fell into his touch, all else melting away as she tasted him, a sensation like coming home after a long absence, the sense of rightness almost shocking before it was burned away by desire. After that, he seemed more storm than man. A force of nature near overwhelming, blinding her to anything but him. She didn't know where the rest of her clothes went or how he had managed to divest himself of his. She didn't know how she got to the bed. All she knew was the need for him, the ache of it between her legs and at her breasts and spiraling through every inch of her.

There was no gentleness to it, and for that she was thankful. She didn't want gentle. Didn't want him to crack her defenses any more than he already had. No, she just needed him to be hers, to drown her in pleasure for a time.

She urged him on with eager hands, pulling him down to her, spreading her legs and catching them around his hips as he kissed her again. He was large, the sheer size and weight of him making her feel delicate in comparison. His cock, as it slipped over her, was large, too. The sensation of hard over soft only fed her need. She arched up to him, but he put one hand on her hip, strong enough to hold her where he wanted her as he feasted on her, making her mindless with him.

Just when she was close to cursing his name for the delicious torture of it, he relented. Moved up over her again and slid home with one certain thrust that had her bowing beneath him with delight. She rode the storm then, let him take her as he willed, too caught up in the pleasure of him to do more than follow his lead. It was wild and fast and noise and fury as they moved together, until finally the pleasure burst and the lightning spiked behind her eyes and she came with his name on her lips like a revelation.

～

Afterward, as they lay panting and replete, side by side on Jean-Paul's huge bed, it took Imogene a few minutes to fight her way clear of the fog of satisfaction and be able to think again. And all she could think was that it would be near impossible to leave his bed when the sun rose and resume being sensible Imogene Carvelle.

She turned onto her side so she could watch him as he lay staring at the ceiling, a smile playing over his face.

"Do you have a question, Lieutenant?" he asked, not moving.

"No. Just looking." There was plenty to see. Naked, he was all grace and muscle. She wanted to run her hands over that body. To get to know it even better. To burn it into her memory.

"I hope you like what you see. Though you may have to grant me a few moments' rest before I can satisfy your urges again." He turned his head on the pillow, eyes alight with amusement.

"My urges are well satisfied," she said softly. "For now." Her heart twinged. Now was all they could have. This night. Perhaps another, though she knew it would be safer if they did not. He was too much. Too overwhelming. Too good at what he did with those big hands and that clever mouth and the rest of him. Too...right.

When he could only be wrong.

Another taste and she might become fatally addicted to something she could never truly have.

He frowned at her then, as if he had some inkling of what she was thinking. "You look overly thoughtful for a woman whose urges have been satisfied," he said, his voice light but cautious.

"Should a woman not think?" she said.

"A woman should do whatever she chooses to do," he said. "And she should not waste a quick mind or clever hands or whatever other skills the goddess may have granted her. But I'd prefer if she looked as though her thoughts were happy ones when she's in my bed. And I thought we took care of your worries back in the palace." He rolled to face her. "Is something wrong?"

"No." She had to catch her breath a second before she could continue the sentence. The pang of anticipated loss grew stronger with that lying "No." Just as well that Jean-Paul wasn't a Truth Seeker, to know lie from honesty when he heard it. She turned her attention to his body again, worried he could read her too clearly if she met his gaze. The light in his bedroom was dim, only two earth-lights above the bed shining down on them. But that soft light gleamed over his skin and played over the muscled planes of his body almost lovingly.

A pretty sight.

As was the elaborate silk embroidery that covered the paneled hangings above the bed and the heavy quilt now half tumbled to the floor. Shades of

blue and golds and green in fantastical sea creatures
and flowers that didn't belong together but com-
bined into something as glorious as the man
himself.

The pale linen sheets set off his olive skin ad-
mirably and highlighted the sheer size of the bed
itself. Undeniably the bedroom of a rich man. A
powerful one. One who would, by happenstance of
his birth, come to wield only more power and play
the games of politics throughout his life. Unless he
did something catastrophically stupid—after all,
nobles did occasionally fall into disgrace—his place
was certain. A place his family had fought and
striven for over centuries, no doubt. But part of the
machinery of the empire. What would he do to
protect it?

"You're not still worrying about Andalyssians,
are you? I told you I spoke to the emperor.
Nothing will happen."

Was it nice to have such certainty? Was that
also a by-product of his sure knowledge of who he
was in the world? It could easily turn to arrogance,
perhaps, but in Jean-Paul, it felt more like solidity.
Like there was a foundation under his feet that
couldn't be shaken, that let him just be who he was.

It almost certainly wasn't that simple, of course.
No one had a perfect life. The lands that belonged
to the du Laqs were large, almost a small kingdom
of their own. Eventually the lives of thousands of
people would be impacted by every decision Jean-
Paul made. That wasn't an easy thing to come to
terms with. Power. She remembered when her
magic had first manifested. How her life had been
uprooted and reformed in an instant. Even though
she'd been raised in the hope that that moment
would come for her, she hadn't been ready for just
how different she would feel. Would she be remade
once more if she bonded with a sanctii?

Perhaps. But this time she would be a little more ready for the change.

She hadn't been ready to meet Jean-Paul. Wasn't ready to acknowledge the true depth of loss she was feeling, knowing she would be gone from his life again in the morning.

In another life, it would have been nice to stand with him on such solid ground and feel such certainty. But looking at him now, she knew, regrets or no regrets, that she had to find solid ground of her own before she could think about sharing it with another. And that other would have to be willing to accept her for who she was. Including accepting her sanctii, should she succeed. And try as she might, she couldn't remember any of her history classes mentioning a duquesse who had a sanctii.

So. Her ground was not his, and he was not to be hers. She would slip away out of his life again. Leave him to find another with that same sense of their place in the world to stand beside him and guard the responsibilities he held. To wield that shared power for good.

She should. And she would. But she could steal a few more hours of him first.

"I hope not."

He smiled at her. "Trust me. All will be well." His hand drifted to her shoulder, skimmed down an arm. "Stay the night," he said. "Or two."

Her foolish heart twinged again. "I can stay tonight. But only that. I have an assignment out of town." She didn't want to tell him what it was. A sanctii was her choice. No one else's opinion mattered.

"So soon?"

"Only for a few weeks."

"When you return, perhaps?" he said. His voice was light, but there was a hopefulness to his tone that only deepened the knife pricking her emotions.

"Oh, you will have met some other pretty face by then." She tried to keep her tone light in return though the words were not easy to say.

"Lieutenant, I think you underestimate your charms."

Damn it. She had underestimated him, that much she couldn't deny. "Maybe. But I cannot ignore the reality of who you are. You're a duq to be, Jean-Paul. I'm a nobody. There's no happy ending to this story."

His expression darkened. "You're not nobody. Don't say that. I—"

She stopped his words with a finger to his lips. "Don't. You can't change my mind. I knew this before I agreed to come here with you tonight. You knew it, too. Neither of us has to like it, but we have to accept it. We are...only what we can be. And what we can be ends when I leave in the morning. So, my lord, you can storm and be angry at me, and I'll leave now and save us the aggravation. Or you can kiss me again and we can take what we've been given and enjoy it a little longer. Your choice."

She could fairly feel the frustration rising off him, the need to argue, to talk her around, to shape the world to how he wanted it to be. She tensed, waiting for the argument. But then she saw him make a choice. Saw him let it go. Let *her* go, perhaps.

"As my lady wishes," he said in a tone not completely free of regret. Then he drew her back down to him and she went, trying to focus only on the joy of his touch and not the dawn that was coming too fast.

Chapter Eighteen

Just one more step.

Imogene stared at the salt circle ringing her and the second circle she'd painstakingly drawn opposite it.

One more step and she would call a familiaris sanctii and bond the creature to her. A goal achieved. A step forward in the life she wanted for herself.

A success.

After two unending weeks of study and preparation for this moment. Hours she'd thrown herself into, both fascinated by the sanctii with each piece of new information she had gained and simultaneously aware she was using that fascination, using her bone-deep certainty that this was what she should do to cloak the equal bone-deep certainty that she missed Jean-Paul like fire every second she let herself think about him.

It didn't matter that she knew it was ridiculous. Didn't matter that she barely knew him. Didn't matter one whit what perfectly rational and logical arguments she came up with to convince herself she'd done the right thing when she'd had crept out of his bed at dawn, gone home to change and pack, and then reported to Colonel Ferritine to tell him

she wanted to take part in the training—and, what
was more, she could leave Lumia early if that would
be useful.

The captain had looked at her oddly for a moment, and she'd wondered if he could somehow tell
where she'd spent the night. Or that she was so
eager to leave the city for reasons other than the
allure of a sanctii. But he had nodded and agreed in
the end, and she'd come here to Cylienne, a small
village in the middle of nowhere. East of Lumia by
several days' carriage ride. Only important in the
scheme of things because of the barracks here that
was used for various training activities. The sanctii
school being one of them. Of course, she hadn't
had to endure several days in a carriage. She'd been
given permission to use the portal at the Cylienne
barracks to make her journey. The others chosen to
attempt a bonding had followed over the next two
days, seven other officers of various ages, though
most, like her, were still only lieutenants. She was
the only woman among them this time. Somehow
that made her only more determined to succeed.

She'd buried herself in the books they told her
to read and practiced everything she had been
taught. She knew the ritual she was about to perform forward and backward and, quite possibly,
could have recited it in her sleep. But that didn't
change the fact that just then, when she should be
focused only on the ritual and the fact that she was
about to summon a sanctii, there was a small part
of her mind wondering what Jean-Paul would think
if he could see her now.

Would he murmur a proud "Well done, Lieutenant," or would he be shocked? Or worse, indif-
ferent, having already forgotten her?

No.

No time to pine over something out of reach.
She needed to think about the sanctii. Once they

made their bond, he would be hers for life—or until she released him. A far more important moment in her life than a night in the bed of a man she still wanted but couldn't have.

She wrenched her thoughts back to the circle and the chamber where she stood. Looked down at the brazier floating in the channel of water between the two circles.

So. A choice. One she could make for herself. One that was hers and hers alone.

She stepped a little closer to the edge of the circle, careful that her boots didn't brush the salt. She wore black breeches with her uniform. A skirt in a circle where one had to move could cause unforeseen accidents.

A breath to center. Another to focus her attention down to nothing but here and now. Then she drew the silver dagger from her belt, lifted her hand to hover over the brazier, then pricked her finger to drip blood into the flames. It was rare to use blood in water magic, but it was water of a kind. And bonds needed to be sealed.

As the drops hit the coals, the tiny sizzle each impact made thrumming through her, she began to speak the words. A steady stream of complex precise commands. At least they were in Illvyan, not the sanctii tongue. That sounded like gravel and ash given voice, and though she had learned more of it in her time at Cylienne, she wasn't adept enough to speak it now while also pouring her power out over the flame and the blood and into the circle beyond.

It took less time than she expected. She was still repeating the words of the ritual for only the second time when a sanctii appeared in the circle beyond her.

She didn't stop talking, didn't so much as allow herself to flinch. The way the sanctii appeared was always startling to a degree. As though human minds could never quite get used to another living being just stepping out of thin air.

The sanctii stood quietly, making no attempt to break the circle. She had been warned that some resisted, but he seemed ...attentive rather than reluctant. The linen—or something near to it—pants and tunic he wore were black, making him appear almost part of the shadows not entirely chased away by the fire. But only almost. He was too solid to be a dream, his body, tall and strong. The arms bared by the tunic were heavily muscled, the skin mottled gray and black that reflected the glow of the brazier coals, the red gleaming over the near silver lines that cut through parts of the gray. The gray tones of his face were broken by a bold slash of black across his eyes, shadowing them even more than usual. A sanctii's eyes were inky black, no whites visible. His reflected the firelight, too, the flashes of red in their depths almost mesmerizing.

But she couldn't afford distraction. She had to complete the ritual.

"What shall I call you?" she asked carefully. The summons should compel him to answer truthfully. To make him give her a name to use to complete the bond. But some sanctii chose not to answer at all. Without the name, there could be no bond. They knew that as well as the mages did. Those who chose to speak were choosing to be bound. No one quite knew why they agreed. Access to the human world seemed to please them in some way they didn't choose to explain.

"Ikarus," the sanctii said. His voice did indeed sound like his throat might be made of rock, but Imogene detected no hesitation in it.

"Ikarus," she repeated. "I am Imogene."

He tilted his head at her. "Female."

"Yes." She had been told to speak truth in the circle. "Does that matter?"

Ikarus shrugged, muscles rolling under his skin. "No difference. Strong magic." That time his voice sounded almost approving.

Satisfaction swept through her. She nodded at the sanctii. "You know what I will ask next?"

That wasn't exactly sticking to the script. Perhaps she would regret it, but he had made no move to attempt to break her magic yet. And she would rather their bond be forged as she meant to continue. With him as a partner to her magic, not just a servant to fetch and carry and perform magical tasks to order as a servant might sweep her room or wash her clothes. He would need to follow orders sometimes, as she herself did, but she wanted an ally, not an enemy compelled.

"Yes," Ikarus replied.

Her hand was still dripping blood into the brazier. She needed to finish this before she did something foolish like grow faint. She straightened her shoulders. Held the sanctii's gaze unflinching. And spoke the words to bind him to her.

Chapter Nineteen

❧❧

I mogene had only been back in her new quarters in the Lumia barracks for an hour when a knock on the door interrupted her unpacking. She hauled herself up from the floor near the chest of drawers she had been filling, wondering if her mother had sent another parcel from Imogene's room at home.

It was expected that those who had newly bonded with a sanctii would live at the barracks for some time. A way of providing breathing space whilst they adjusted to the bond and learning to work with a sanctii. Her parents, who she had visited as soon as she had returned from Cylienne, had reacted much as she had expected they would to her announcement that she had bonded with Ikarus. Her father had looked surprised, then proud. Her mother surprised, then alarmed. Then annoyed. A daughter with a sanctii was a very different kettle of fish when it came to the marriage mart.

Imogene had almost been able to see the wheels turning behind her mother's narrowed eyes—no doubt reforming her plans for Imogene's social life for the next few months. Her mother had been no more pleased by the news that Imogene would be living in the barracks for the foreseeable future. Imogene hoped devoutly that she would be sent on another assignment before she had to return home to live. That might give her mother time enough to calm down. Or Imogene time enough to find a home of her own if her mother couldn't reconcile herself to this new reality.

Her mother had insisted on helping Imogene pack, and then there had already been an additional package of embroidered wall hangings waiting when Imogene had arrived with her trunks far later in the day than she had expected to return. Why her mother thought she might want to hang a delicate floral embroidery in an army barracks was beyond her. But she recognized the gift as the beginning of a peace offering perhaps, even if it was one she had little use for.

The room she was allotted as a lieutenant didn't fit much more than a bed, an armoire, a tiny worn armchair, and a small table with two chairs. Officers were allowed to make the accommodations more comfortable, but she wanted to do it her way. Her taste was not her mother's. If this was another parcel from her mother, she hoped it would contain food rather than furnishings.

But when she opened the door, it was no courier waiting with package in hand. Instead, the hallway was very full of Jean-Paul.

So much so she made a stupid noise of surprise, prompting Ikarus to say [Come?] in her head.

[No,] she replied silently. She'd grown used to the form of wordless communication the sanctii could use over distances all too quickly. It was comforting to know that Ikarus was there if she needed him, could hear her, wherever he may be. [I'm fine.]

But she should talk to the man standing before her rather than the sanctii. "Major du Laq," she said cautiously. "What can I do for you?"

"You didn't tell me you were back." He smiled, and her heart kicked.

She had to fight the urge to smile back. What was he doing here? She had made herself clear. She'd told him they had no future. Then she'd left him while he was sleeping. Not to mention left the city altogether.

She shouldn't want to smile at him. Perhaps she needed to be clearer with herself, too.

"I only just arrived," she said. Then realized he might take that to mean she'd had every intention of contacting him. "And I wasn't aware that you expected to be informed of my whereabouts, Major." She glanced past him into the hallway. So far they were alone, but there were six other lieutenants living on this floor. One of them could arrive at any moment. She needed Jean-Paul to leave.

His smile didn't falter. "Ah, yes, about that. I've decided that your idea was a bad one." He stepped fractionally closer. She held her ground, though his scent made her head spin, the memory of his touch flooding her senses.

"My idea?"

"That we should end things. That was a terrible idea, Imogene. I have missed you these last two weeks. More than I care to admit, frankly. Your commanding officer wouldn't tell me where you had gone. I did, however, hear that the latest cohort from Cylienne would be returning today. I took a chance that perhaps that was where you were and, therefore, that you might have returned."

There was no point lying about it. And certainly the news that she was now bonded might work to change his mind about their future. "It was."

"And am I to offer congratulations on a successful venture?" He looked as though he actually meant the words.

"If you are asking if I bonded a sanctii, then yes, I did. His name is Ikarus. Would you like to meet him?" She lifted her chin. Jean-Paul merely shook his head, expression unchanged.

"Not just yet, perhaps," he said. "But congratulations, Lieutenant. You are a woman of more talents than I knew, it seems." He smiled, head tilting. "You didn't tell me you had won the chance to do this."

"It didn't seem relevant," she said. "I didn't think I would see you again, other than in a professional capacity should our paths cross, perhaps." There. Blunt enough.

"It seems, Lieutenant, that you have found it easy to put me from your mind."

No I haven't. She bit back the words. Swallowed. "There seems little point in yearning for something beyond my reach."

"Such a logical answer. Are you sure you are not, at heart, an ingenier like your father after all, Lieutenant? Does logic rule all?"

His eyes were locked on hers, the gray depths of them a color she could get swept away in. If she was so foolish as to let herself fall.

"Did you not think of me while you were away? Were your thoughts only for the sanctii and what came after him? Tell me that is true, Lieutenant, and I shall walk away."

I didn't miss you. Four short words. She could speak them and it would be over. A simple lie. Best for both of them. But somehow, she couldn't lie to him. She wanted to give him the truth. She could offer that much. But not here in the hallway where anyone could come across them, having what could only look like a lovers' quarrel.

Chapter Twenty

I mogene stepped back from the door, waved him inside. Closed the door again after he crossed the threshold with three determined strides and pressed her palm to it to set her wards to work so they wouldn't be interrupted. Or overheard. Then she turned to face Jean-Paul, who stood, muscles tense, eyes intent, filling the small room with his presence without even speaking.

"I can't tell you that's true," she said. "I did think of you. There is something between us. Something that could have been. But nothing has changed. You are a noble. You'll be a duq. I'm a lieutenant. With a sanctii. I am not the woman you will marry. And I will not be anything less. I won't be a temporary thing, a pause while your family wears you down to choosing one of the oh-so-suitable noble daughters of the court. It hurt to leave your bed, and that it hurt was terrifying. I do not do this, Jean-Paul. I do not let myself—" She hesitated.

The words that sprang to mind were "fall in love," but that was too big a truth to let slip. Too big to acknowledge, even. Love at first sight was a concept she had thought only true of the romantic tales in novels. She was, indeed, too much her father's daughter to believe in it, let alone do it. She had told herself that she would be sensible when it came to her heart. That she wanted a career. To travel the empire. So she could give up a more normal life of marriage and children. Or find a man who would support her choices should she want to. Choose with care based on friendship and chemistry.

Not in the blink of an eye and a chance encounter in a ballroom. No one did that.

"Grow attached so fast," she continued. "But it would hurt more to have you again, knowing there can only be another ending."

He watched her as she spoke, gray gaze locked on hers. She had the curious feeling that she might as well have been landing a blow with each word, though he didn't flinch or interrupt or look away. Instead he just watched, as though he was committing her to memory.

One to be treasured when he left her behind, perhaps.

She let the silence hang, not knowing what else to say. No words that would come easily over the burn of denial in her throat and the regret chilling her gut. The last few days, caught up in Ikarus, in the rush of power and delight that came with the sanctii, she had convinced herself that she was forgetting this man. That had been untrue. But she would forget him with time. She had to.

"Ah, but Imogene, what if there didn't have to be an ending?" he said.

She felt her mouth drop open. For someone like him, those words meant only one thing. Marriage. "You're going to be a duq."

One corner of his mouth lifted. "I know. It is a nuisance. But it is not the only thing I am. I am a man, too. A man who knows what he wants."

"Your family would never agree." She still

couldn't get her mind around the idea. Let alone say the word "marriage" out loud.

"They may take some persuading, true." He shrugged. "But my father raised me to know what I want and to do what I think is right. He may not like learning that his lessons have stuck well when it comes to this, but he will not stand in my way. I want you, Imogene. My life is not full of many things I can truly choose for myself. I think my wife should be one of them."

Had it grown hot in the room? "Even if your family agreed, the court...I was not raised to be a duquesse, to run a grand estate." She waved a helpless hand at him. "I like my job. I'm not ready to give it up."

"I would not ask you to. Not entirely. We have time. My father is not yet old, and he is healthy." There was that certainty again. That tone of believing he could will whatever he wanted into being. It was seductive.

"I have a sanctii," she said. "Has there even been a duquesse with a sanctii?"

"If I have no problem with it, it should not bother anyone else. As I see it, it is an asset to the family, not a liability." He grinned at her then. "And a reminder that I would be a foolish man to mistreat a wife who holds such an asset."

"Were you intending to mistreat your wife?" she asked, breathless. Trying for a joke to lighten the sense that her world was once more spinning around her, perchance to settle in an entirely new order.

He shook his head. "Never," he said fiercely. "What is mine, I protect. I am enough of a du Laq to know that is true. I would keep you safe, Imogene. You can go, be a diplomat, wield that mind and magic yours in service to the emperor. You can have your sanctii. And I will stand ready for you when you return."

Oh, she wanted to believe him. What would her life be like if she could believe him? But it seemed impossible. "This is fast, Jean-Paul," she said. "I need time. You need time. We've barely met."

"As I said, we have time. There doesn't have to be a grand announcement yet. No betrothal ball with half the city in attendance. But I would like to try, Imogene. I think that together, we would be a force to be reckoned with. And that apart neither of us will be truly happy."

"How would we do that?" she asked, knowing she—despite all the protests of logic and reason—wanted to say yes. To throw her life onto a completely new path so she could walk with him.

His smile was pure joy. "As to that, Lieutenant. I came to invite you to a ball."

Chapter Twenty-One

Imogene still wasn't convinced she wasn't dreaming when she found herself once more waltzing with Jean-Paul in the emperor's ballroom four nights after her return from Cylienne. It had been a dizzying week, between continuing her work with Ikarus and Jean-Paul discreetly putting himself in her path at every opportunity. She hadn't yet returned to his bed. She was trying to be smart. To wait a little and see what happened when they got to know each other better.

But with his hand holding hers and his body close enough for her to feel the heat of him, she wasn't sure how long she could resist.

She tried to distract herself with the other dancers, to enjoy the whirl and spectacle of them. Her third imperial ball in a month. Hardly what she had expected when she had returned from Reyshaka. The Imogene then would have laughed at the thought of taking so much as a step in the direction of a duq-to-be, let alone agreeing to contemplate marrying one.

But she couldn't regret choosing Jean-Paul, even if she was baffled as to how exactly he had come to lodge himself so deeply into her affections in so little time. The simple truth was that her heart lifted with joy every time she saw him, and she liked him more with every moment they stole together. Those might become harder to steal. He had said he would introduce her to his parents tonight.

The thought of that was enough to make her palms clammy, and she was grateful when the music came to an end, giving her a chance to catch her breath.

"You're thinking too loudly again, Lieutenant," Jean-Paul said as he escorted her off the floor. "And though I find your face deep in thought enchanting, I would like to see your smile. It's a ball. You're wearing a gown that I find deeply fascinating." He cast a quick glance toward the swooping neckline of the emerald brocade dress she was practically stitched into. "Let us enjoy the night."

"That's easy for you to say. You're not meeting my father tonight," Imogene said. And even if he had been, her father was unlikely to express the same concerns as to his suitability that she knew, despite Jean-Paul's assurances, his father would have about hers.

Just thinking about it made her stomach flip.

[Patterns.] Ikarus's voice was a rumble in her head.

[What patterns?] she replied, attention still half in the ballroom.

[Humans. Music.]

[Dancing?] Then she halted. [Wait. You're here? We discussed that.]

[You said not be seen. Not to stay away.]

She flushed. That was true. She should have been more careful with her words. She wasn't part of the Imperial Guard, and they were the only people who could call a sanctii in the emperor's ballroom without causing an uproar. Of course, if a situation arose where the Imperial Guard needed

to summon a sanctii, there would be an uproar regardless.

[You must not be seen,] she reiterated in her
head.

A snort of agreement, as though telling her he
knew very well how to behave, was all the reply she
got. It wasn't entirely what she had expected, this
sanctii business. There was more give-and-take.
More...friendship.

Friends with a sanctii and engaged to a duq.
Strange days.

Her attention came back to the ballroom, and
she realized Jean-Paul was leading her toward the
imperial party. The duq was not the only important
man she would meet tonight. She was to be formally introduced to the emperor—she couldn't
quite bring herself to think of him as just Aristides,
as Jean-Paul seemed to—as well. But that didn't
feel quite so intimidating.

And sure enough, when she curtsied for the emperor and empress and rose again, she felt far
calmer than she had been expecting to.

"Lieutenant Carvelle," Aristides said, his voice
smooth. "We are pleased to meet you." His gaze
flicked to Jean-Paul, who stood behind her. "The
major speaks highly of you."

He looked somewhat entertained. Was he
pleased that Jean-Paul was...involved? Would he
remain pleased if he knew one of his future duqs
wanted to marry someone like her? And what in
the name of the goddess had Jean-Paul been saying
to the emperor? It would be a horrendous breach
of protocol to turn her back on the emperor and
roll her eyes at Jean-Paul, but she was tempted. But
she resisted the urge and offered a murmured
"Thank you, Your Imperial Highness."

She caught the gaze of the empress seated beside her husband. She also looked amused, a dimple

flickering in her cheek. Her dress was the shade of a new anden leaf, a color that flattered the bright green of her eyes. It was draped to hide her stomach, and the gold leaves rioting over the bodice were placed to draw the eye away, too, but there was no mistaking that there would be another imperial prince or princess sometime in the fall. The crown prince was not yet eighteen. His youngest sister only six. Five children. Imogene couldn't imagine it. And yet Liane looked younger than Aristides, though they were close in age. Perhaps she had a touch of the illusioner's art.

"Your dress is lovely," the empress said.

Kind of her, Imogene thought. Her dress was beautiful, but simple, relying on line and drape and the beauty of the floral brocade to overcome the lack of expensive lace and embroidery and jewels that decorated the gowns of the nobles. Imogene's mother's clothier was very good, but there was still a limit to what any dressmaker could do without the unlimited funds required to produce clothes like the empress wore.

"Thank you, Your Imperial Highness." She curtsied again and back up a few steps, hoping Jean-Paul might join in the conversation. She could think of nothing just then that seemed like suitable conversation for an empress.

He seemed to take the cue and moved to stand beside her. But before he could add anything to the conversation, there was a slight commotion from behind the emperor. A door opened in the wall behind them, and three black-clad Imperial Guards walked through ahead of a group of four Andalyssians. Including, Imogene saw, her stomach sinking, the Ashmeiser.

Chapter Twenty-Two

"**D**amn," she muttered under her breath. Part of her wanted to turn, and leave. But she stood her ground. The emperor knew who she was. She'd been approved to attend the ball. And she knew she had done nothing wrong.

Still, she hoped the Ashmeiser might fail to recognize her.

No such luck. The man had no sooner straightened from his bow to the emperor and empress, his robes still settling back into their elaborate folds, when he caught sight of Imogene and raised a blond brow. He looked from her to Jean-Paul and then moved to join them.

"Lieutenant...Caravalle?" he said, pausing before them.

She curtsied. "My lord Ashmeiser. It's Lieutenant Carvelle."

"Close," he replied. He had unusual eyes for an Andalyssian—the color of frosted water. A light blue gray that held no hint of human warmth. "Illvyan names sound similar to my ears. You will forgive my poor grasp of your language."

His grasp of Illvyan was excellent. She knew that from experience. Still, she managed to drag

the Andalyssian equivalent of "No need to apologize" from the depths of her memory.

The words only gained her another assessing
look. "You are keeping exalted company, Lieutenant. You are not on duty, I think?" He turned to
Jean-Paul. "Are you and the lieutenant friends, my
lord?"

"We are," Jean-Paul said firmly. "I thought your
delegation had decided to rest tonight rather than
attend the ball, my lord."

He sounded somewhat exasperated to Imogene's ear. And not bothering to take much care to
hide it. She tried to gather her thoughts, to pivot
from meeting the empress to being the diplomat
she was learning to be. But the Ashmeiser's robes
carried that faint mossy salt-smoke aroma she asso-
ciated with their court. Here in Illvya it seemed
even earthier. Almost...unpleasant. The storm of
memories it conjured threw her off her stride.

"We changed our minds," the Ashmeiser said.
"We have been finding your balls so entertaining,
after all, my lord. It is helpful to learn of the tradi-
tions of Illvya more thoroughly so we can use that
knowledge to build a bridge more strongly between
our two countries."

Imogene doubted the Ashmeiser had ever found a
ball entertaining in his life. No, he seemed more like
the type who might take pleasure in dissecting some
small helpless furry animal. Or an enemy. The back of
her neck crawled as the smoke filled her nostrils. If
they hadn't been invited to join the ball, why had they?
It was somewhat rude. For one thing, the servants
would be scrambling now behind the scenes to make
sure the arrangements for the supper that would be
served later included options for the Andalyssians.
Not to mention redoing most of the seating order.

She could only hope she was seated away from

the Andalyssians. Because the smoke smell of the Ashmeiser was making her stomach roll.

Thankfully the Ashmeiser turned back to join the rest of his countrymen. Imogene caught the empress's eyes, and Liane grimaced behind the Ashmeiser's back, the expression so fleeting, Imogene thought she might have imagined it. Apparently she wasn't the only one who disliked Andalyssians. A comforting thought.

She looked up at Jean-Paul. He was watching the Andalyssians, paying attention to their interactions. She had to learn to enjoy this, she realized. If she married Jean-Paul and joined the court, she had to find meaning in the politics, a way to work for good with it, or she would go mad. Perhaps a start would be to view tonight as an exercise the tutors in the Diplomatic Corps had set her to study. How to meet an emperor, the embodiment of an old failure, and your future father-in-law all in one night, and emerge unscathed.

She rather thought that seemed an unfair degree of difficulty for one night. But there she was. Still smelling smoke and ash, still not ready to meet the Duq of Saint-Pierre and somehow manage to convince him she would be a good match for her son.

But then Jean-Paul looked back down at her and smiled, and she remembered why she was doing this. Which made her want to roll her eyes at herself even as she acknowledged the emotion.

"Would you like to dance again before I find my father?" Jean-Paul murmured. "Encounters with the Ashmeiser require a palate cleanser, I find. Normally I would choose ilvsoir, but it's early in the evening to start drinking hard liquor." He smiled again. "Besides, you are far more intoxicating than ilvsoir in that dress."

As he was intoxicating in his evening clothes.

But she wouldn't have said no to a slug of the sharp sweetness of ilvsoir to take the sting of smoke out of her throat either. Why was it lingering? The Ashmeiser really hadn't smelled so strongly of it.

A memory twinged. A religious service in Deephilm. Priests of earth performing magic and ritual she hadn't understood. She'd tried to watch what they were doing, but the power was blurry to her eyes, half hidden in fog. But she remembered how sharp the taste of ash had been in her throat as they'd worked their rite.

Wait.

She swung back toward the Ashmeiser, opened her eyes to the magic, reaching for the ley line beneath the palace. The Ashmeiser blurred before her eyes, as though there was a veil of smoke around him. Was he using magic? Here, so close to the emperor?

Even as she watched, he stretched an arm toward Aristides, hand held at a peculiar angle.

"Stop!" Imogene yelled, fear spiking through her. And before she could even form the next thought, Ikarus appeared, wrapping one large hand around the Ashmeiser's arm and dragging him away from the emperor.

Everything dissolved into chaos. Guards appeared from every angle. People started yelling, the Ashmeiser one of them. The emperor, she noticed, had moved first to put himself between the empress and the rest of the room, though his gaze was on the Andalyssians. Other than that, the details grew distance as she stared at Ikarus, feeling as though she was witnessing something not quite real.

Until Jean-Paul said, "Imogene, could you ask Ikarus to let the Ashmeiser go, please."

As she did so and Ikarus vanished from sight, everyone turned and began shouting at her.

Chapter Twenty-Three

"What were you thinking?" Jean-Paul said, raking a hand through his hair until long strands broke free of the ribbon confining it. He'd stood by Imogene's side as the storm had broken over her head, but after the emperor had eventually said, "Enough," and turned to start placating the Ashmeiser, he hustled her out of the ballroom and into another of the endless small meeting rooms lining the corridors. The silence in the tiny room was startling. Her breath rang in her ears, and she could hear Jean-Paul breathing hard, too.

"Imogene?" he repeated. "Answer me."

Imogene bristled. "I was thinking that the Ashmeiser was using magic in the emperor's presence. And he was hiding it." Her cheeks were hot, but the rest of her was ice. Shock, she supposed. She'd called a sanctii into the emperor's presence without permission. The Ashmeiser had put on a grand show of outrage that he'd been treated so badly. There was no evidence he'd done anything at all, nothing to warrant the emperor pushing the boundaries of diplomatic protection. She'd made a mistake, it seemed. A terrible mistake. In front of the emperor. In front of Jean-Paul. Who, instead of trying to help her, was yelling at her as all the others had. Her eyes stung, and she gritted her teeth. She would not compound her error.

"Their magic is different," Jean-Paul said. "It feels different."

Was he actually going to lecture her on Andalyssian magic? "I know," she said, wrestling her voice to calm with an effort. "I have been to Andalyssia. I have studied their ways. So perhaps you could grant me the courtesy of not talking to me like I am a child, Major."

His brows drew down. "I'm not—"

"You are," she said. "And I don't appreciate it."

"You made a mistake," he said. "Even if he was using magic, calling Ikarus was...hasty."

He was trying to be calm, it seemed. To talk rationally. But she could see the muscle clenched at his jaw and the fire in his eyes. He was angry. And somehow his emotion only amplified hers.

"Perhaps. I breached protocol, certainly, and I'll wear the consequences of my actions. But I won't be condescended to by you. If you want a wife to talk down to, then I am not the woman for the job."

He scowled at that. "You called a bloody sanctii in the middle of the emperor's ball. You assaulted a diplomat. Allow me a moment to catch my breath."

"No," she said sharply. "I won't. Because you haven't allowed me to catch mine. You said you protect what's yours. So do I. I'm sworn to protect the emperor. Maybe I made an error of judgment tonight, but I'd do it again if I had to. I made a mistake, yes, but I would remind you that I wouldn't have been in the position to make that mistake if you hadn't pushed me to be here tonight."

Part of her knew that was an unfair charge to

bring against him. But part of her also knew there was truth to it. He was pressing her. Hurrying her. Attempting to sweep her off her feet, to shape the world his way.

"You're saying this is my fault?" It was close to a shout, disbelief and frustration warring in his voice.

She threw up her hands. "I don't know! But you're pushing too fast. And I can't think. And I won't make a choice this way, Jean-Paul. It's not fair of you. Or to you. Or to me."

"What are you saying?"

"That I need some time. Alone. I need you to leave me alone."

~

"You cannot be serious about that girl." Andre du Laq stepped into his son's path as Jean-Paul reached the entrance to the ballroom.

"Father, now is not the time." He was in no mood for a lecture, still reeling from watching Imogene stalk away from him after their fight, fury clear in the rigid line of her back and the swish of her skirts. And getting into an argument about her with his father would only make this night more of a disaster.

"It is," Andre said tightly. "I was willing to indulge you in this, to meet with this lieutenant who seems to have snared your attention somehow, but I must put my foot down. The girl has no control. A duquesse needs finesse. Tact. Judgment."

"Imogene has all those things."

"Yet she called a sanctii in the midst of the emperor's ball?" Andre sounded incredulous.

Jean-Paul hid a wince, thinking of how he'd said as much to Imogene only minutes ago. "She's young. She's only just bonded the sanctii. You know that can be difficult to navigate."

"Yet you thought it was wise to bring her here tonight. Maybe she's not the only one who lacks judgment." Andre frowned. "Did she tell you she intended to bond a sanctii?"

"No. And that is irrelevant." She had thought they had no chance when she'd made that choice. Perhaps she'd been right.

"Do you want a wife so impulsive? One who is a stronger mage than you? That's a dangerous thing, Jean-Paul."

"I want a wife who is a partner," Jean-Paul said. "Whose strengths complement mine. And one who I hope I would never inspire to use her strengths against me."

"Best try not to startle her, then," Andre snapped. "I need you to use your brain here, my son. Stop thinking with your cock and consider your legacy. The responsibilities of a duquesse are vast. Noblewomen are educated from birth to take on such positions. What does an ingenier's daughter know of running a great house? Of duty and tradition? Of politics? You need a girl like Celadin. And yes, I understand that she may not be the one for you, but she is not the only suitable girl at court. Be smart, Jean-Paul. Pick one of them."

"And if I don't? What will you do, Father? Disown me?" He was trying to rein in his temper, but he could feel it sliding from his grasp. He curled a hand into a fist at his side, trying to calm himself. Imogene had left. He had said stupid things. She had done something reckless to incite them, yes, but he could have handled it better. Because she'd left. And she'd asked him not to follow her. Or speak to her. So why was he even fighting with his father at all? Why risk fracturing this relationship, too, when Imogene may have just taken herself out of his life entirely? He didn't know.

His father didn't seem to know either. Andre

hesitated a moment, then shook his head. "Don't force my hand, Jean-Paul. Use your brain. And go in there and clean up the mess you made."

Chapter Twenty-Four

Invisibility was tiring. Imogene, having endured close to a week of it already, was growing thoroughly sick of the whole thing. She'd taken the lectures on her stupidity, she'd taken being temporarily removed from any duty other than her continuing lessons with Ikarus and being ordered to stay in the barracks the rest of the time, and she'd taken the not-so-subtle avoidance of her classmates who only now spoke to her if it was part of one of the lessons, as though they were worried that screwing up might be contagious.

The army, apparently, had decided that the best place for her was out of sight. Colonel Ferritine had given her a lecture on responsibilities that made her ears ring. But he'd followed it up with more gentle advice to just wait for things to pass.

Which she was doing. For the second time. The first time, after the mission to Andalyssia, her disgrace hadn't been her fault. This time, it was. That didn't make it any easier to bear. She wondered if it had been the sheer boredom of being punished that had led Alexei Berain to resign after Andalyssia.

She could take that option. Give up her commission. Go and work with her father. Build a different life. Ikarus would be useful to her as an ingenier, too. They couldn't take him away from her, at least, though she was under strict orders to keep him under control. Which was unfair. He had done precisely as she had asked in the ballroom and then stopped and left as soon as she had asked again. Her control over her sanctii was fine. It was her control over herself that was the issue.

Jean-Paul, too, it seemed, had taken her at her word. He hadn't contacted her. Which left her in the increasingly irritating position of being annoyed by getting exactly what she'd asked for. She would have to make the first move. Which she might do if she was surer that he hadn't just wiped his hands of her entirely, thanking the goddess for a lucky escape from a bad choice.

Even if she hadn't been full of doubt, she hadn't been given permission to leave the palace grounds.

So she was dutifully making her way back from the training halls to her quarters once more, thinking of dinner in her room and more study before she slept, when she passed the gate to one of the palace gardens. One that was technically not off-limits to anyone living within the palace's boundaries. And technically still on the way back to the barracks.

Surely no one would begrudge her a few minutes' peace admiring some flowers and drinking in the afternoon sunshine before she returned to her punishment? If they did, they could hardly make things worse unless they did decide to kick her out. She'd never heard of anyone being cashiered over flowers, though. So she grasped the gate and pushed it open.

She was admiring a bank of bright pink roses when a voice from behind her said, "Lieutenant Carvelle?"

A female voice. One she recognized. Heart

sinking, she turned and saw her suspicions confirmed. She sank into a curtsy at Empress Liane's feet, cursing her luck in her head. The empress was the last person—except perhaps the emperor himself—she wanted to see.

"Get up. It's too hot for that," Liane said. She fanned herself with one hand. "Don't have babies in summer, Lieutenant. I've done it twice. Learn from my errors."

"Do you need to sit, Your Imperial Highness?" Imogene asked, alarmed. Bad enough that she had run into the empress—an encounter that would no doubt bring her more lectures if anyone from the barracks saw them—but it would be worse still were she to have some sort of complication to her pregnancy with Imogene in her presence.

Liane grimaced, still fanning. "I've been sitting half the day. I wanted to stretch my legs."

"Where are your guards?" Imogene scanned the garden. The empress was alone. Not so much as a lady-in-waiting accompanying her. That had to be rare.

"I told them to leave me alone. I'm sure there are half a dozen sanctii nearby"—Liane waved a hand at the air irritably—"but apparently I was fierce enough to chase everyone else out of eyesight. Rank is useful sometimes. And rank plus pregnancy is also useful. Remember that, too." She rubbed the pale blue silk of her dress where it stretched over her belly.

"I will leave you alone," Imogene said, taking a step backward. The empress had private gardens she could walk in, of course. But if she wanted this one, well, Imogene might be willing to risk the wrath of her commanding officer but not her empress.

"No, stay. I keep asking Aristides about you. To make sure you were being treated fairly. So far the only answer I get is 'it's an army matter.'" She shook her head. "Men. They are irritating when they get pedantic about stupid rules." She linked an arm through Imogene's. "Walk with me. And tell me they haven't been too hard on you."

"I'm fine, Your Imperial Highness. I did break the rules, after all. I can take my punishment."

"You acted to protect my husband and myself," the empress retorted. "I would prefer to see such behavior encouraged in the court. But I will not interfere if you prefer to play by their rules." Bright green eyes twinkled at her. "But if they grow tiresome, you are welcome to let me know."

Imogene imagined how well that would go down with Colonel Ferritine. Having strings pulled in her favor would probably ensure she got sent to the dullest post in Illvya for a year. If not two.

"I am fine, Your Imperial Highness" she repeated. "Let's admire the flowers."

Chapter Twenty-Five

They walked, the empress moving slowly, her movements awkward when she bent to sniff a bloom here and there. "What about Jean-Paul?" Liane said. "Aristides said he thought you might be our next Duquesse of San Pierre. Before all this fuss. Jean-Paul is a good man. Don't let this nonsense scare you off if he is the one you want."

"It's a big decision to take on something like that," Imogene said slowly. "We still have only known each other a short time."

Liane laughed. "Well, I can understand that. I almost ran away before my wedding. But I'd known Aristides a long time. And I loved him. So I stayed. And became an empress. Which sometimes seems ridiculous, even now. But we adjust. And love is worth the adjustment, my dear." She rubbed her belly again. "And a little discomfort." She paused, pressing her hand into her back. "I swear this boy is kicking my kidneys on purpose."

"It's a boy?"

"So the healers tell me." Liane smiled. "I wouldn't have minded either way." She squeezed Imogene's arm. "I think he's telling me that I've walked far enough for now. Come, walk with me back to the rose garden. We can have tea. It's nice to talk to someone new."

"I'm supposed to return to my barracks."

The empress grinned wickedly. "Imogene, I outrank every one of your commanding officers. Tell them to come and see me if they wish to complain about you being late."

Put that way, she couldn't argue. "The empress made me do it" was an excuse no one could argue with. She laughed at the thought of the look she would get from Colonel Ferritine at that one. "Thank you, Your Imperial Highness. Tea would be lovely."

When they reached the rose garden, there was already a small table set for two, a linen half tent set to shade it from the sun. It seemed the sanctii guarding the empress could also relay her desire for tea to the palace servants.

Liane sat with a grateful sigh. "At least the Andalyssians are leaving the day after tomorrow," she said. "That will stop all the tedious dinners we've been holding for them. I don't mind the balls—I can avoid them at the balls—but the Ashmeiser Elannon is not my idea of a sparkling conversationalist at dinner."

"No," Imogene agreed. "He is not."

"You've been to Andalyssia, I understand. What's it like?"

Imogene told her about the court and the country while they waited for tea.

Liane listened and asked intelligent questions in the right places with an ease that made Imogene feel envious. The empress had obviously honed the skill of making people feel at ease and welcome as well as any diplomat. But then the nobles had to

work the tools of politics too. Imogene might not
have been born to be a duquesse but maybe—if indeed she was still to be one—her training in the
corps would give her some small grounding on
which to build.

By the time the servants arrived with a tea service and a trolley laden with more food than the
two of them could possibly eat, Liane had deployed
her charms so well that Imogene was halfway to
forgetting Liane was the empress and just enjoying
her company.

The servants moved everything to the table
with efficient grace, then faded back out of
eyeshot.

Imogene reached for the teapot. It was her
place to serve the empress. Her hand brushed the
silver and her nose filled with the scent of moss-
laden smoke. She jerked her hand back in-
stinctively.

"Imogene?" Liane said, "Is something wrong?"
She reached toward the teapot, and Imogene
knocked her hand away.

One of the servants sprang forward but Liane
said, "Wait." The servant stopped by the empress's
side. Both of them stared at Imogene, who was
frozen with horror.

Goddess. She'd laid hands on the empress. She
was ruined. But she had gone this far. She had to
see it through. Salt ash stung her throat and filled
her nose and she fought the urge to call Ikarus, to
get him to take the teapot away. "Don't touch
that."

"Why not?" Liane's gaze was sharp.

"You might think I'm crazy," Imogene said. "I
may well *be* crazy. But it smells like Andalyssian
magic to me. There's something wrong with it."

"My food is tested," Liane said, in a tone that
was too calm. She sat farther back in her chair,

moving cautiously as though afraid the teapot might explode.

"Their magic is strange. It's hard to notice for an Illvyan. It can blur things. It's..." She struggled to find the words. "Imagine air and earth magic mixed somehow. It always felt odd to me."

Liane sat back in her chair, looking pale. Then she turned and said to the servant, "Fetch me my husband, Major Perrine, and Healer Terrisse." She paused a moment. "Send someone to find Major du Laq, too. And tell the guard to keep the Andalyssians in their quarters for now. They are not to leave the palace." She smiled at Imogene, the expression sharp and fierce, though she was still pale. "Let us get to the bottom of this once and for all."

It probably took no more than ten minutes before Aristides, the healer, and the major arrived. But it felt like an eternity as Imogene sat and stared at the teapot, wondering if it was about to ruin her entire career. But the healer held a hand over the pot, and her polite interest turned to alarm. "Poison," she said. "An especially deadly one. Brewed from an herb that only grows in cold countries, Your Imperial Highness." She leaned over Liane, studying the empress's face. "You didn't touch the pot, did you?"

Liane had pushed her chair farther away from the table at the word "poison." She was nearly as white as the cloth covering the table. "No, Lieutenant Carvelle stopped me. She saved me."

Aristides reached for his wife's hand, held it tight, both of them staring at Imogene.

"Did you touch it?" The healer's worried brown eyes fastened on Imogene, too. "Let me see your hand."

Imogene's mouth dried as she realized why the healer was concerned. "I only brushed it for a moment." But she held out her hand obediently. It shook slightly. "It feels fine." Would she feel it, though?

"It would. The poison doesn't burn. It's dangerous because it does little until it enters your blood stream. Then you die quickly." The healer bent closer and peered at Imogene's hand. She cocked her head. "How long has it been?"

"Ten minutes, maybe?" Imogene said, heart thumping. Was that too soon to know?

"You're still alive. I think you are in no danger. It acts faster than that on the skin." Terrisse swung back to the emperor and Major Perrine, who both looked grim. "I suggest you send for a Truth Seeker. Start with the servants, though I doubt this is a poison anyone would find easy to obtain in Illvya. So I'd be speaking to the Andalyssians. The lieutenant here just saved the empress's life. And your son's."

Chapter Twenty-Six

"I suppose you will want to marry the girl after all now," Andre du Laq said to Jean-Paul the next morning as a servant poured coffee into their cups. The invitation he'd received from his father asking him to join his parents for breakfast had been written more as a command. Jean-Paul, who'd been caught up in the interrogations all night and had been planning on sleeping for an hour and then bathing and going in search of Imogene, had instead presented himself at the duq's townhouse.

The breakfast, he knew, would be excellent. Normally, it wouldn't have been enough to convince him to appear. But learning what his father's current stance on Imogene might be was necessary if he was to go to Imogene and convince her to give him another chance.

He hadn't gotten near her yesterday. A servant had found him at the barracks and brought him to the emperor's audience room, where a young blond Truth Seeker had already been asking questions of the Andalyssians.

Imogene had been standing with the empress, who looked pale and furious, and she had barely spared him a glance before focusing back on the Truth Seeker.

Who was very good at his job and had soon made it clear that the Ashmeiser was in the plot up to his neck despite the Andalyssians' strident protests to the contrary.

At that revelation, the empress had stepped forward and said, "I've heard enough. I believe you all owe Lieutenant Carvelle an apology. But that can come in due course. You can all clean up this mess." She'd waved a dismissive hand at the Andalyssians. "The lieutenant can come with me. We never did get tea." She paused, one hand on her belly. "I will deal with her colonel."

Then she'd looped her arm through Imogene's and left.

Jean-Paul had had the mad urge to run after them before Aristides had said, "She will wait. This will not." Which was true but truth had not made it easier to force his mind to duty rather than Imogene.

But sitting with his father and mother both smiling at him, he wasn't at all certain that Aristides had been right. Or that Imogene would forgive him. He gazed down at his coffee, unable to summon any appetite though he knew he needed food to make up for his lack of sleep.

"Well, Jean-Paul," his mother asked, "am I to have a daughter-in-law at last?"

He grimaced. "I think, Mother, that that is yet to be determined." He swigged coffee.

"She has the right stuff, that one," his father said with a sly smile.

Jean-Paul paused mid sip. "That's not what you said after the ball."

"I've changed my mind. Your mother always tells me the ability to change one's mind is a sign of wisdom. She is loyal to the crown. And brave enough to speak up, even though if she'd been wrong, she would have ruined her career, most likely."

More likely his father's ability to adjust his opinion with a smile and act as though he'd never felt any differently came from years of diplomacy and politics. Would he end up like that, too? He'd prefer the wisdom-based kind of decision-making himself. But he was, at least, wise enough not to try to dissuade his father from his newly found approval of Imogene. He merely rolled his eyes at his father.

"Poison. Cowardly, if you ask me," Andre continued. "If you want to kill a man, shoot him or stab him or something. More cowardly still to go after a pregnant woman." His expression twisted in disgust. "We should set half their damned country on fire."

Andre was clearly fully informed about everything that had happened at the palace. As he usually was. Luckily, Jean-Paul didn't think Aristides would choose violence as revenge. More likely, he'd just make the Andalyssians pay through the nose while he rooted out the heart of the discontent in their country via more subtle means. Diplomacy wasn't always gentler than war.

"But back to your lieutenant," his father continued. "Loyalty, bravery and magic. That's a start. You say she has a brain. We can teach her the rest. And the court will become used to the sanctii, I guess. She's not the only water mage about." Andre sat back, looking satisfied. Then he smirked at Jean-Paul. "So all you have to do is get her to say yes."

Chapter Twenty-Seven

Imogene was half asleep when the empress's carriage drew to a halt outside the barracks. Liane had insisted on calling a carriage to deliver Imogen back to quarters—which was ridiculous when it took as long to drive through the winding palace roads to get from the palace to the administrative buildings as it did to walk through the grounds. But Liane, Imogene was learning, didn't take no for an answer often. Perhaps that came with being an empress. She'd insisted Imogene spend the night at the palace. Not that a luxurious bed in a palace guest suite had made it any easier to sleep. Imogene had been too overwhelmed by everything that had happened to rest.

Ikarus appeared at one point to sit with her, as though keeping watch. He'd gone again when she'd climbed into the high bed an hour or so before dawn. But she hadn't slept long. Which was why she was yawning now. Colonel Ferritine had asked her to come see him at eleven after Liane had finished telling him that Imogene's punishments were to be over and done with immediately, and she was to be given all due consideration for her next assignment, and the empress would be writing a commendation for her bravery.

It was nearly quarter to eleven now.

But as she stepped out of the carriage, she spotted Jean-Paul looming on the steps once more, looking like a storm cloud in his uniform.

Her heart lurched, and had it not been for the firm grip of the driver who had insisted on offering her a hand to help her down, she may have stumbled at the sight of him.

She stood for a moment, gathering her wits. Not fast enough, because it gave him time to walk to her.

"Lieutenant, good morning," he said. He looked almost as rumpled as she felt. He hadn't shaved, and his uniform was wrinkled. Hers was pressed and clean via the magic of palace servants who had managed the feat in the few hours she had slept, but she still felt disheveled and unsettled.

"Good morning." The response was automatic. As was the smile that followed it. She had missed him. She'd wanted to talk to him last night but hadn't been able to figure out how short of sending Ikarus to find him. That might have been pushing her newly reinstated favor a little too far.

"I know you said to stay away, but I wanted to make sure you—" He broke off, as though he was uncertain what to say, eyes searching her face.

"That I what, Major?" she said gently.

"That you knew that I know I behaved like an idiot at the ball. I was angry, but not at you. I shouldn't have spoken to you that way. I apologize. I wanted to give you the space you asked for. And I will leave again and give you that space if it's still what you want, but Liane said yesterday that we all owed you an apology, and that is true. And I wanted mine to be the first. I didn't trust you as I should have. I told you I would protect you, and I didn't. There's no excuse. But I am sorry. And it won't happen again. I miss you. But I will go, if you still need time." He moved to step backward.

Her hand shot out and grabbed his arm, fingers curling into the wool of his uniform jacket. "Don't."

He looked down at her hand, hope breaking over his face. "Does this mean I'm forgiven?"

She wasn't sure about that. But she *was* sure she didn't want him to go. "I'm thinking about it," she said, smiling.

He smiled back, hope silvering his gray eyes. "What can I do to make you think faster?"

"Not much. I have to be in the colonel's office in about five minutes."

"I already spoke to the colonel. He said to tell you that he had something come up. He'll see you this afternoon."

"That was very confident of you," she said, lifting a brow at him.

He shrugged unapologetically. "I prefer hopeful. But even if you sent me away, I figured you might be as short on sleep as I am."

"Do you need a nap, Major?" she asked.

"Is that an invitation?" His voice did that low and rumbling thing that made her want to kiss him.

"I haven't said I've forgiven you yet."

"I could convince you if we took a nap." He wiggled his dark brows.

A sound came from the driver that she thought might be a stifled laugh. A reminder they were having this conversation in broad daylight. While standing outside the place where she still would be working after today, Jean-Paul or not.

She stepped back from him. "Perhaps we can compromise with a carriage drive? Find somewhere to talk."

"Excellent plan," Jean Paul said. He reached

past her and opened the carriage door again. "The empress won't mind if we take her carriage for a spin. She has several of them. And I would like to talk to you. About whatever you'd like to talk about." He held out a hand so she could step back into the carriage. "My father thinks I should definitely marry you," he said just as she put a foot on the step.

She almost banged her head on the top of the door as she jerked in surprise but managed to recover and climb inside. Jean-Paul followed. Really, the man was far too nimble for his size. He was annoyingly good at too many things. The thought made her annoyingly happy.

"I thought we were going to take our time about this?"

"We may be," Jean-Paul said. "But I warn you, my father is impatient. And very good at getting his own way."

"Like father, like son, it seems," she said.

Life as a du Laq, she was beginning to think, would definitely never be dull. She might fit right in, in fact. She rather liked the thought of learning how to be very good at getting her own way when she needed to. Perhaps she should start practicing. Because she knew what she wanted. And that was the man sitting opposite her, grinning like temptation and trying to be on his best behavior. Every overly large, overly confident, aristo, brilliant, handsome inch of him.

"You never actually asked me the question," she pointed out.

"I was giving you time and space," he said. "Do you still need them?"

"A little," she said. "I quite like this apologizing part. I may need a little more."

"I can do that," he agreed cheerfully. "As often as you need me to. And then?"

She smiled, charmed by him all over again. And hopelessly in love. "And then, if you ask very nicely, I think it likely I will say yes."

Epilogue

❦

He had asked very nicely, Imogene reminded herself as she surveyed yet another ballroom two months later. And she had said yes. She didn't regret it, not for a second, but, as she was learning, it took hard work to become the kind of duquesse-in-waiting she wanted to be. She had a lot to learn. Luckily, Jean-Paul's parents were determined to help her. As was the man himself. Who was the reason she was standing here, sipping water rather than campenois because she had been given strict instruction from both her mama and the duquesse that it would be unsuitable to become tipsy at one's own betrothal ball.

The du Laqs had spared no expense. As many members of the court as could be squeezed into their ballroom were here. The house at Sanct de Sangre, their country estate, was large, but it wasn't as large as the palace. The emperor and empress were not here, but only because Liane had given birth two days earlier to a healthy baby boy. Liane had sent the extravagant sapphire earrings Imogene wore as an apology for not being able to attend. And the necklace that matched them as a betrothal gift. Imogene suspected the jewels were worth more than her parents' house. They were extraordi-

narily beautiful, but she wasn't yet easy with
wearing half a fortune around her throat.

"Can you believe this is finally happening?"
Chloe said, standing beside her. She sipped campenois happily, her brown eyes sparkling as brightly
as Imogene's necklace.

"What do you mean, finally? It's only been two
months." Time had whirled by far too quickly for
her. She'd barely had time to catch her breath,
caught up in Jean-Paul and Ikarus and the changes
in her life. "Little more than three since I met the
man."

"True," Chloe said. "But you've been doing
duquesse school for weeks. Between that and wedding planning and the army, I'll be glad when
tonight is over and you have some time back."

Imogene didn't have the heart to tell Chloe she
wasn't entirely sure that was going to happen. Yes,
they agreed to no wedding for a year. But duquesse
school showed no signs of letting up. And she
wanted to go on at least one more mission before
the wedding. Somewhere warm this time.

"I'll be glad when we get through the formal
part and I can have some of that campenois you're
downing."

Chloe smirked and lifted her glass again. "Rank
comes with responsibilities." She scanned the
crowd, waving her glass at the assembled masses.
"There's certainly a lot of them, aren't there?"

"Indeed," Imogene agreed. Chloe had gone
above and beyond to join Imogene at many of the
parties and balls and gatherings Imogene was attending as part of her introduction to the court,
but she still had her own responsibilities and
couldn't be out every night. "I'm not yet convinced
they don't multiply overnight." An effect only amplified by the Sanct de Sangre ballroom, which was
walled in mirrors, making the crowd appear infi-

nite. The effect made her vaguely queasy. It was hard enough to keep them straight without having to sort reflections from reality.

She was starting to find friends amongst the court and to make sense of the information about its members being crammed into her head. But none of them would replace Chloe. So the court was just going to have to get used to Imogene's choice of best friend.

"Do you know who that is?" Chloe asked, tilting her fan discreetly to her right.

Imogene followed the direction of the fan and Chloe's gaze. The young man standing at the foot of the staircase, wearing a coat in a blazing shade of blue, was handsome in a way that bordered on pretty in its perfection. His dark hair was artfully arranged, and his blue eyes flashed as boldly as his jacket. She was sure she had met him during one of the relentless series of dinners and parties she had been attending in Jean-Paul's company, part of the du Laq "bring Imogene up to speed" campaign. She searched through the list of names she'd been committing to memory, seeking to match it with his face. It came to her soon enough.

"That's Charl de Montesse. He is nephew to the...Marq of Verneile, I believe." And good friends with the intense blond Truth Seeker who had questioned the Andalyssians. He, Imogene had been surprised to learn, was the heir to the Marq of Castaigne. And one of the many aristos Imogene had met in the last two months since she had saved the empress. Chloe wouldn't be particularly interested in who Charl was, but Imogene begun to grow used to thinking about where people slotted into the court. "Would you like me to introduce you?"

Chloe grinned at her, head only turning briefly to meet Imogene's gaze before turning back to watch Charl. "He's pretty. Yes, please."

"Very well." Imogene led Chloe across the room, performed the introduction, made polite small talk with Charl and Chloe until she was sure Chloe could handle the rest on her own, and then went in search of Jean-Paul. The formal part of the evening would commence shortly, and she wanted a moment to stand with him and remind herself why she was making this choice all over again.

She found him eventually, in one of the side chambers, speaking to Barteau, the du Laqs' seneschal. "Are you hiding from me, Major?" she said as his face lit at the sight of her.

"From everyone but you," he said. "Have I told you how beautiful you look tonight, Lieutenant?"

"You have, but you can tell me again." She turned slowly so he could admire the dress. Its design had been an act of diplomacy in itself, one that had taken weeks. Imogene's mama, after her initial stunned surprise when she'd been told that her daughter was to become a duquesse, had risen to the challenge and wasn't afraid to match wits with the duquesse fencing deftly over the details of the wedding as though she'd been born noble herself.

Tonight's dress seemed to be the topic of most debate. A fact which made Imogene nervous to contemplate how long it might take when it came to choosing her actual wedding gown. Both the duquesse and Imogene's mama held strong opinions over what was appropriate. White for a betrothal, of course, but then there had been other colors to consider. The du Laqs' were gold and blue, but the Carvelles didn't have any rank to warrant a crest or family colors. Which complicated deciding what needed to be incorporated into the design.

The clothier had, after exercising so much patience that Imogene was going to have to get Jean-Paul to pay her extra, suggested silver to represent the metal of Imogene's father's work and pale blue and green for her magic. There were tiny beaded cog wheels and quills to represent the words of diplomacy—amongst the rioting flowers embroidered over the bodice and spilling down the skirt. They made her smile every time she found a new one. Jean-Paul had promised to kiss every one before he let her take off the gown tonight. She was looking forward to it. Much as she was looking forward to wearing the ring Jean-Paul had chosen with her. Gold and silver weighed down with a multitude of perfect sapphires and diamonds, set into the band so she could wear it safely during her work. He'd promised her a second more ostentatious one for when they needed to dazzle the court. Just what he considered ostentatious was daunting to contemplate. But rings and dresses were minor details.

The promise she was about to make was what was important. The promise and the man she would be giving it to.

She came back to face him. Her future. Her heart. She hadn't been looking for him, and it might not always be an easy thing that she had found him, but he was hers.

"You are beautiful," he said. "Always. I love you, Imogene Carvelle."

"I love you, Jean-Paul du Laq." She stretched up to kiss him fast, then broke away before they could get carried away and ruin the dress or her hair or anything else. She kept hold of his hand, though. "So let's go tell the world."

THE END

Bonus epilogue

✦❦✦

She looked liked a duquesse, she just wasn't sure how long it might take before she actually felt like one. Or if, indeed, she ever would. Months and months of lessons from her future in-laws, and Jean-Paul helping wherever possible, and she'd begun to feel like she might have a grasp of the basics. But, like magic, the minutiae of court politics and court protocol was a process that took years of study to master. Which was why the children of the aristo families learned these things from birth, along with the more mundane matters of spelling and history and arithmetic and such.

Memorizing names and lineages made her head ache worse than even the dullest lessons she'd ever endured at the Academe.

But she wanted Jean-Paul, and so she had to take what came with him. That was the bargain she had made.

Even if it seemed impossible at times.

She sighed and took a step closer to the mirror, careful not to move too fast. Her satin shoes had heels that were higher than was wise when she had to steer a wedding dress that was structured and hooped and adorned to within an inch of its life and weighed nearly as much as she did. But the shoes had been deemed suitable and necessary to lessen the height difference between her and Jean-Paul at the altar. Given Jean-Paul was one of the tallest men at court, she didn't think an extra inch of heel was going to help much. She wasn't short, but her betrothed made nearly everybody look smaller than they were.

Having survived the careful step, she fussed with her necklace. It would be a lie to claim that she hated the part of the bargain that came with a near unlimited budget for clothing and whatever else her heart might desire. Or that access to a collection of truly breathtaking jewelry acquired over centuries was unpleasant.

The design negotiations over her wedding gown had been as bad as the betrothal dress. She'd assumed it might be simpler, given the betrothal dress had dealt with issues of family symbols and colors. But the marriage of a duq-to-be was a matter of state, and the wedding dress had to shine. She'd never been to a coronation or an Imperial wedding, but she'd seen the paintings of the dresses Empress Liane had worn for both those occasions, and they weren't so far removed from the one she wore now.

A stark reminder that it didn't really matter what she and Jean-Paul thought about their wedding, they had little control over the formal parts of today.

She was trying not to think about it. Better to focus only on Jean-Paul, who would be waiting for her when she reached the temple's altar.

Of course, to reach him and the safety of his hand over hers, she had to walk past about a thousand guests—most of the court—and then even more family connections of the du Laqs. Her own guest list accounted for maybe fifty. Which seemed far too few friendly faces to get her through the day. Chloe was her chief attendant, so that was one ally close, but it was still two against hundreds.

All those aristo eyes watching her. She'd gotten a little more used to it over the months of practice, but it was still a daunting prospect, knowing some of those watching didn't wish her joy of her day. Rather, they were hoping she might make an idiot of herself, or at least commit some small blunder that would give them even the smallest political leverage over Jean-Paul or his father.

That was why her dress had to be perfect, and her hair, and the jewels that turned her into a fair semblance of a glass ornament. The dress was embroidered with metal threads in the same colors as her betrothal gown, mingled with hints of the du Laq blue and gold. But the heavy satin was also scattered with pearls and small brilliants that echoed the priceless fire from the diamonds she wore. The tiara woven into her hair and the earrings and necklace were exquisite but hardly subtle. If a stray sunbeam hit her during the ceremony, she might well blind unwary onlookers. The thought made her giggle. It was one way to defeat the scrutiny of the court.

She flexed her hands, which were, apart from her betrothal ring, unadorned. She'd put her foot down on the matter of additional rings, insisting that she would wear Jean-Paul's and no other.

But even his ring felt weighty and unfamiliar now that she was standing alone in the dressing room at the temple near the palace. The largest one in all Illvya. Where Domina Francis herself, the head of the entire temple in the Empire, would marry them.

Imogene had never expected her wedding to be a public spectacle. Truthfully, she hadn't thought much of a wedding at all, her focus on her magic and her career she'd worked so hard for. All that time and effort. Jean-Paul had promised that she would still be one of the Imperial mages after they wed. Indeed, she had been on several shorter missions in the last few months. His parents had tried to protest at first, but Jean-Paul had overridden their concerns.

He was sincere in his support, she knew, but she wasn't sure that his will alone would be enough to shift the weight of royal tradition and protocol that would also expect her to become a fixture at court. Thank the goddess that Jean-Paul wasn't actually the duq yet. There'd be a far smaller chance of her escaping any of it if he'd already held the title. Which was why she needed to make sure she started now and established herself in the mages while his father was still alive. Privately she wished her father-in-law to be a very, very long and happy life.

If she worked from the beginning, then by the time—far in the future—when Jean-Paul took up the title, her career would be just part of who she was. Unusual perhaps, for a duquesse, but she could live with being different. She was different to the other duquesses. For a start, she had a sanctii.

"Ikarus," she whispered. "Are you here?"

"Yes," the sanctii said, appearing beside her. His black eyes studied her for a long moment. "Worried? Why?"

He was sensing her nerves. Their bond was growing more complex every day.

"It's a big day," she said. "Lots of fuss."

"Humans," he rumbled, tone somewhat dismissive. As far as she could tell, sanctii seemed to find humans largely entertaining, their day-to-day concerns largely unimportant. Perhaps they bonded with human mages purely so they could observe more closely? Or maybe they liked to have the chance to be part of the entertainment.

"Is it simpler for sanctii? Having a mate?" she asked, adjusting the necklace again.

He shrugged. "Different."

She wouldn't get any more than that out of him. Sanctii females were rare in the human world. Only a few had been bonded over the long centuries of Illvyan history. Which left the mages with little insight into how sanctii society functioned. And the sanctii themselves were tight-lipped on the matter. Clearly more sanctii were created somehow. And they had two sexes. But no one had learned more than that. Today wasn't the day to push for information.

"How do I look?" she asked him. Foolish, really. A sanctii didn't view human clothes and fashions in the same way.

But to her surprise, Ikarus looked her up and down. "Good," he said. "Mate be happy." One corner of his mouth turned up.

He seemed to like Jean-Paul, which made life easier. And Jean-Paul had grown used to him too.

"I hope so," she muttered, staring into the mirror one last time. "Will you stay for the wedding?"

"Stay," Ikarus agreed. But then he vanished again as a knock came at the door.

"Come in," she said, thinking it would be her parents or Chloe come to tell her it was time to start. But the person who appeared behind her in the mirror was Jean-Paul. She turned faster than was sensible in the gown and overbalanced. She wobbled, then regained her footing. "What are you doing here?"

"I came to see you," Jean-Paul said.

"You're supposed to be downstairs, on display, so everyone can make bad jokes as they arrive," Imogene said. But her nerves were melting away as she took him in. He wore a formal uniform in the du Lac colors rather than the black of the Imperial army. Deep blue, but instead of yellow, the braiding and buttons and embroidery that decorated the shoulders and cuffs and edges of the jacket were actual gold that shone almost as bright as her diamonds. How many hours had his manservant had spent polishing them yesterday?

"Everyone can wait," Jean-Paul rumbled as he stared down at her, a smile playing over his mouth. "We will have little enough time together today until this production comes to a close. I wanted a chance to be alone with you."

There was a look in his eyes as he took in her dress that suggested he approved. She held up a warning hand. "You cannot muss me. There's not enough time to fix my hair and you'll be a widower before midnight if your mother discovers that I wrinkled this dress before I get down the aisle."

"My arms are long," he pointed out. "I can reach you without mussing you."

She looked down at the skirt doubtfully. It belled out around her for several feet in every direction. "You can muss me later," she said. "When it's official."

He laughed. "I seem to remember I've mussed you unofficially often enough."

"Then holding off this one time won't hurt you," she retorted. But her resolve weakened. He was very handsome in his uniform, and the joy in his eyes as he looked at her made her melt a little, as it always did.

"One kiss," he said, holding up a finger. "Just one. A reminder why you're going through with this nonsense instead of running from the building as any sensible woman would do."

"Oh, there are any number of women downstairs who'd happily take my place without fleeing," she said.

"None of them light my days, though, my love," he said. "So I need to be sure I light yours too."

He did. Every overly tall, overly sure of himself, overly aristo inch of him. He was hers. She was his. And maybe he was right. The vows they would make in the temple, under all those eyes, were to make everyone else happy. What mattered was the vows they made for each other.

She reached out her hands, and he took them, inching closer so the gleaming toes of his boots just touched the edge of her hem. The feel of his fingers wrapped around hers, made her dizzy for an instant before she focused back on his storm colored eyes.

"Let's say them now," she said.

He looked a little confused. "Say what?"

"The vows. What we're going to say to each other downstairs. Marry me, Jean-Paul. Just you and me."

"Lieutenant, I like the way you think." His grip tightened, and he cleared his throat. "But isn't there usually a domina involved?"

She rolled her eyes at him. "Not doing anything we can't do ourselves. And anyway, if we miss something, they'll take care of it downstairs. But I want this to be just for us. Everything else is theater and spectacle. This is the part that means something."

"All right." He cleared his throat again, looking charmingly nervous for just a moment. "I believe it's the wife who starts."

She smiled. "Jean-Paul Gerrald Henri Louis du Laq."

"Impressive," he murmured.

"Sssh. You have too many names, but I know them all." She started again. "Jean-Paul Gerrald Henri Louis. Today I make this vow. To be yours body and blood. To make my heart's home with you. To offer my strength as solace, my fidelity as fire, my—" She hesitated as a sudden rush of happiness caught the words in her throat and she had to blink back tears. "My breath as my bond. May our love grow strong as the Tree of the World, its roots as deep. And may we not be parted until the goddess grants that to the earth we return."

Jean-Paul's eyes were full of emotion, the storms threaded with silver light, like the sun breaking through. His tone was steady and certain, rumbling with a sound that lit her heart as he began. "Imogene Sera Carvelle. Today I make this vow. To be yours body and blood. To offer my strength as shield, my fidelity as fire."

The words seemed to ring in the air, filling her ears and her heart.

"My breath as my bond. May our love grow strong as the Tree of the World, its roots as deep. And may we not be parted until the goddess grants that to the earth we return."

They stared at each other, lost in the moment.

"So, do you feel married now?" Jean-Paul asked.

"Do you?"

One side of his mouth lifted. "I do, wife."

"So do I." Strange, how a few short sentences could change her world all over again.

Then she started to laugh, too happy to do anything else.

Jean-Paul laughed too. Then shook his head. "So, can I kiss you now, wife?"

"Just once," she said. "Then we have to go downstairs and put on a show."

Jean-Paul leaned closer, one hand cupping her cheek. His lips on hers were soft but fierce, and she felt heat flare as it always did. What he did to her, this man. What he was. It was worth all the nonsense. She was almost about to throw caution to the winds and tug him closer when he pulled back, expression regretful.

"My mother will absolutely murder us both if I crush your dress." He sighed. "Do we really have to bother with the official part? As pretty as that dress is, I'd much rather see you out of it."

She laughed. "I'm afraid so, my lord. So you should go take your place. The sooner we start, the sooner it will be over."

He nodded, grinning foolishly. "True enough. So, wife. I will see you soon. To marry you. Again."

THE END (AGAIN)

Chloe's story continues in The Exile's Curse, book 1 of the Daughter of Ravens series. It's set after the Four Arts series which is the first Four Arts trilogy, starting with The Shattered Court.

A note from M.J.

I hope you loved reading COURTING THE WITCH. I had so much fun writing my Four Arts series that I had to write a prequel. If you've picked up this novella and haven't read the Four Arts, then THE SHATTERED COURT is where all the fun begins (read on for an excerpt). Or if you want to find out more about Chloe, then THE EXILE'S CURSE continues her story after the Four Arts trilogy ends. You can read it without reading The Four Arts trilogy.

As an indie author, it really helps me when readers get the word out about my books, so if you enjoyed the book, please consider leaving a review at the store where you purchased it and tell your friends!

If you want to stay up to date with all my news, find out about new releases and sales, then please sign up to my newsletter at www.mjscott.net.

About the Author

M.J Scott is an unrepentant bookworm. Luckily she grew up in a family that fed her a properly varied diet of books and these days is surrounded by people who are understanding of her story addiction. When not wrestling one of her own stories to the ground, she can generally be found reading someone else's. Her other distractions include yarn, cat butlering, dark chocolate, and watercolour. She also writes contemporary romance as Melanie Scott.

You can keep email M.J. at mel@mjscott.net or follow her on:

Also by M.J. Scott

Fire Kin

Romance (writing as Melanie Scott)

The Cloud Bay series

Don't Blame Me

Right Where You Left Me

You Belong With Me

The New York Saints series

The Devil in Denim

Angel in Armani

Lawless in Leather

Playing Hard

Playing Fast

Acknowledgments

Writing a book during a pandemic is odd. I feel like I should be thanking Zoom, Wifi and streaming services for keeping us all semi-sane. But thank you to the Fantasy Realms gang for inviting me to be part of the anthology that resulted in this novella, thank you to Robyn and Sarah for story wrangling, my awesome crit gals for support and shenanigans, my Mum who is always there for me and the Diva Kitty for general good catting and keeping me company.

Excerpt from The Shattered Court

"Milady, please pay attention."

It was precisely the last thing she wanted to do.

For a second, Sophie Kendall rebelled, lingering where she was, hands pressed into the pale gray skirts of her dress, no doubt wrinkling the silk. She had a sudden wild urge to bolt through the half-open glass doors and flee. But then her good sense, or at least her sense of resignation, returned, and she forced herself to turn away and smile apologetically at her tutor.

"But they're playing so well." She looked back over her shoulder at the two teams of young men playing round-ball on the Indigo Lawn outside the doors, envy biting. Oh, to be so free. Here in the palace she wouldn't be able to join in the game. Proper young ladies, let alone ladies-in-waiting, didn't play round-ball at court. But she could, at least, sit and watch. Or she could if she ever had the luxury of nothing to do.

Just an hour or two to herself in the sunshine. Was that too much to ask for?

She couldn't remember the last time she'd had a spare hour or two alone. And right now she couldn't imagine when she might next do so.

Captain Turner's bushy white eyebrows drew

together, but his expression was kind. "Milady, your twenty-first birthday is in two days. There will be plenty of time for frivolity then. But now you need to learn this." He gestured to the large leather book on the table in front of him. "Your Ais-Seann is not a trivial matter. Do I need to remind you that you're—"

"Thirty-second in line to the throne, about to come into my birthright if I have one," Sophie said. "I know the speech, Captain. It's just . . ." *I want to be more than Lady Sophia Kendall, valuable brood-mare.* But proper young ladies didn't say such things out loud. At times, being a proper young lady was enough to make her want to scream.

"It's such a nice day," she continued, trying not to sound too impatient. Sunlight streamed through the windows, making the lesson room seem dull in comparison. The breeze coming through the outer doors was just strong enough to carry the scent of grass and the early-blooming blossoms and possi-bility into the room. It made her skin itch. It made her want to tell the royal family and the court and everyone else weighing her down with expectation to go to hell. Made her want to run far, far away.

But the captain's face showed no sympathy for the restlessness she'd been feeling all day, and she doubted he'd show any actual sympathy if she tried a grander rebellion like leaving the room. Most likely he'd just send a squad of the guard after her to carry her back.

The king, the crown princess, and several hun-dred years of Anglese tradition wanted her pre-pared for her Ais-Seann, so she would be prepared for her Ais-Seann. Her Age of Beginning. Begin-ning of adulthood. Beginning, possibly, of magic. Beginning of many things she wasn't entirely sure she wanted to begin.

If indeed she proved to have any magic, her

power would be dedicated to the goddess with all the proper rites and her person married off promptly to whichever nobleman the king thought best. A royal witch was a prize for the men of the court, and the stronger she was, the higher ranked and more influential the noble to whom she would be wed would be. Not that any of the available high lords of the court struck her as men she was longing to spend her life with. Most of them were fifteen or twenty years older than her, for a start.

If she turned out *not* to have any power, she'd be married off less promptly to some more obscure lordling and might at least get to leave Kingswell and the relentless mores and rules of the court.

The lesser of two evils, just. Maybe. She wasn't entirely sure. Her hands began twining in her skirts again, and she forced them to relax.

There was nothing to be done to protest her fate or escape from it. She didn't have any control over whether she was going to manifest magic, and she'd been schooled from birth to take her place in the court and the society of Anglion. She just wasn't entirely sure why, when she'd known since she was old enough to understand what would happen when she turned twenty-one, it was becoming harder and harder to meekly accept with each passing hour. Perhaps it was just nerves.

Perhaps everything would be perfectly fine if she just kept putting one foot in front of the other and did as she was asked to do. So, like a proper young lady, she smoothed her skirts where her hands had gripped them and sat back down next to the captain.

"I know this seems tedious, child," he said. "But you need to know how to control your magic if it comes in. Royal witches are strong, and we can't predict how your gift will behave when it manifests."

"You can't predict that it will manifest at all," Sophie said, trying not to let irritation shade her words.

"Given your bloodlines, there is a high probability that you will have power, Lady Sophia."

"Much good that will do me," Sophie muttered. One hand strayed to the silver-gray pearl hanging from the slender chain at her throat. *Salt protect me. Lady give me light.* Her thumb rubbed the surface of the pearl again, the smoothness a comfort, though she still missed the uneven texture of the strand of five natural pearls she'd worn for as long as she could remember. But they were a creamy white, and as long as the princess was in half mourning, her ladies couldn't wear white.

The gray had been a gift from the princess herself. Its color alone made it expensive, more than Sophie's family could afford. It was not as darkly beautiful as the rope of black pearls Princess Eloisa herself wore. But then again, Eloisa's pearls could have bought Sophie's family estates many times over.

A true symbol of her family's wealth. And Eloisa's power. Both mundane and magical.

The princess was the strongest royal witch yet living. Magic hadn't ruined her life.

But Sophie was not the crown princess. Magic would bring a woman of her rank only unwelcome attention and an even more narrowly prescribed life: Performing the seasonal rituals. Keeping the water sources blessed. Tending to her husband's lands or the court's as demanded. Earth witchery was hardly exciting. Useful, in a prosaic sort of way, being able to coax crops and animals into fruitfulness and supposedly anchor the prosperity of the court and the country. But hardly exciting.

Once royal witches had been able to do more, to call the weather and do other things only hinted at in the history books. But it had been long years since any royal witch of Anglion had been able to do such things. Eloisa was the strongest living royal witch, and she was gifted with wards and healing and, so it was said, foretelling, but she couldn't, as far as Sophie knew, move so much as a puff of air.

She'd asked her mother once, long ago, why royal witches no longer did such things. Her mother, possessed of only a little power herself, had said that no one knew. Her father, overhearing, had muttered something about inbreeding but then laughed when her mother had told him not to be an idiot.

Privately, since coming to court, Sophie had decided that maybe they just never got the chance to try to do anything exciting. Royal witches were carefully hemmed in with rules and protocol so that their powers served the Crown as the Crown wished to be served. And after that, they served the goddess and her church. It didn't leave much time for trying to tame lightning. And with the pampered court life, there was really no need to try for more.

She tried to imagine the look on Captain Turner's face if she asked him what she would need to do to call lightning. He would probably have apoplexy. And then possibly march her straight to the temple for a lecture on the proper uses of earth magic. She sighed, finger and thumb rubbing the pearl again. It was disappointing to think that actually doing earth magic, or the variety she would be allowed—if she was even able—would be even less exciting than learning the theory.

The captain cleared his throat, drawing her attention back to him. "Maybe magic will be of more use to you than you realize."

"It's not as though I'll be allowed to do anything

useful with it. Witches don't fight battles or anything."

He lifted the book they had been studying. "You've been talking to the crown princess again. Earth magic keeps Anglion prosperous. Feeds our people. Fighting battles isn't everything, milady."

"I believe your fellow soldiers in the Red Guard would disagree with you, Captain. And it's difficult to avoid talking to Princess Eloisa when I'm one of her la-dies." The princess, widowed just over a year, had certain views about marriage and the role that women should play in the court. Views that were not exactly conventional. She had, so far, avoided being wed again. Sophie wondered just how long past her mourning time Eloisa would continue to get away with that. Her father doted on her, but he also wasn't a man to waste a prize in his possession. Not one that could be traded for strength and loy-alty. Or he hadn't been before his recent illness. He was recovering from the sickness that had gripped him most of the winter and spring, but there were whispers in the court that he was weakened for life.

Captain Turner laughed beside her, a friendly deep, rumbly laugh, at odds with his stern weather-carved face. "Maybe so. Still, you won't need to fight battles, milady. No one crosses a royal witch. No one sensible, at least."

That made her smile, unwilling as she was. She picked up her notebook and tried to remember the last thing the captain had said about grounding to a ley line. She knew the theory off by heart. After all, she had been schooled in the history and tenets of earth magic and the lore of the goddess since she was fifteen. Captain Turner was charged with en-suring that those lessons were retained. She thought it strange that a Red Guard battle mage was the chosen instructor for potential royal witches, but that was what the temple had decreed.

She also had regular sessions with temple priors, but they always stuck to the lore of the goddess and wouldn't discuss earth magic. She'd even had one nerve-racking session with the icily formidable Domina Skey, who was in charge of the King- swell temple and therefore also in charge of all of Anglion when it came to matters of the goddess. But Sophie hadn't learned anything new from her. Anything she hadn't learned by now, well, it seemed that it was just about too late.

Of course, amongst that learning was a large hole about the actual rites undertaken by a royal witch—that information being deemed unsuitable for those without power to know of—which seemed entirely unfair. But that was another improper thought for young ladies. Until her power manifested, all she was allowed to know was the foundational theories of magic developed by the temple. The ones that underpinned all three branches of power. And there was nothing she could do about that, either. "All right, Captain. We have another hour. The princess asked me to attend her at midday."